CW00822524

Reuniting With DESIRE

WHO ARE THEY NOW?
A BRIGHTON HIGH SCHOOL REUNION

BRE ROSE

Copyright © 2023 by Bre Rose

All rights reserved.

No portion of this book may be reproduced in any
form without written permission from the publisher or
author, except as permitted by U.S. copyright law, or
for the use of brief quotations in a review. This is a
work of fiction. Names, characters, businesses, places
and events are either used in a fictitious manner or a
product of the author's imagination. Any resemblance
to actual persons or actual events is purely
coincidental.

Editing by Shayna Turpin

Paperback formatting by Whitnay Edes

Cover by Whitnay Edes

The Brighton High School Reunion features twelve stories from twelve different authors. From fun rom-coms to dark and twisty romances, there's something for everyone in this collection.
What has everyone been up to since High School? Where are they now? To take a journey with them and follow along through the Brighton world in each book.
Although this is a shared world, each author has put their special mark on Brighton High School's Reunion. Characters may overlap, but each author's interpretation is unique.

Brighton High School 10 Year Reunion Series

Pretty Reckless by: Em Torrey

Color Outside The Lines by: M. Bonnet

Faking Perfection by: Shayna Astor

The Last Key by: Bethany Monaco Smith

Queen Of Vengeance by: Poppy Jacobson

Reuniting With Desire by: Bre Rose

Up In Smoke by: Cassie Lein

Four Simple Rules by: Aly Beck

Settling The Score by: Lyric Nicole

Damaged Goods by: MK Robert

Infinite Dreams by: Raja Savage

Original Flame by: Whitnay Edes

Author Note

The Brighton High School Reunion features twelve stories from twelve different authors. From fun romcoms to dark and twisty romances, there's something for everyone in this collection. What has everyone been up to since High School? Where are they now? Take a journey with them and follow along through the Brighton world in each book. Although this is a shared world, each author has put their special mark on Brighton High School's Reunion. Characters may overlap, but each author's interpretation is unique.

Please note that the main characters from Reuniting With Desire and Up In Smoke are best friends. There are crossovers in numerous scenes with the same scene being seen from different perspectives. So that the stories stay consistent, certain pieces of dialogue used by Cassie Lein have been copied with the permission of the author, so there is no plagiarism.

As a final note, we are all human. Even though this book has been through Alpha, Beta, Edited and proofread several times, errors always seem to slip by. If any are found, please reach out to Bre Rose or Shayna Turpin so that we may correct them quickly and efficiently without hindering anyone from reading and enjoying. You can reach either of us on Facebook or you can email me at breroseauthor@gmail.com

As always, I love hearing from you. If you want to reach out and scream, tell me what you thought, then please feel free to do so.

Happy reading.

Trigger Warning & Tropes

This is a contemporary dark MMF romance. This story contains dark content so please be sure to check the content warnings and tropes below. If any of these are something you are not able to read, then please stop now. Your mental health is more important to me.

Bullying both in HS and as Adults

Physical abuse

Domestic Violence

Pregnancy misinformation

BDSM/Kink/ Edging/ Sexual Toys

MM relationship prior to adding of 3rd party

Explicit sexual content and physical abuse

Reference to abortion although it never happened

Second Chance

Friends to lovers

Parental death

Unprotected sex

Sex industry workers

Dedication

This book is dedicated to any person who felt like they never fit in high school. Just remember, it's a stepping stone to finding out who you truly are and finding those friends who are more than just a season.

PROLOGUE

DOMINIC

October 2009 Freshman Year

"What's the matter, you whiny ass little bitch, can't handle it?" Abel laughs as Luke and Duke both hold one of my legs, dunking my head in and out of the toilet. I thought using the bathroom during the middle of the last period of the day meant I would be safe. I was wrong. I made it a few steps in before I saw them all standing around smoking, and I knew I was in trouble. Turning quickly, I tried to run away, but they were faster. I made it to the door before they slammed it shut, trapping me inside.

"Please put me down," I beg, but it falls on deaf ears. They shove my head right back into the nasty ass bowl of water and flush the toilet. The rushing of water hits me and there's no time to close my mouth and hold my breath before the water overtakes me, causing the assholes to laugh harder.

"Come on, Abel, let him down now. We need to get out of here before the bell rings. The pussy is too scared to say anything," Rowan's voice rings out. It's only when they pull me up again, my eyes painfully flying open as I'm gasping for air, do I notice him leaning against the wall. He casually takes a drag on his cigarette as he takes in the scene before him.

"Yeah, we need to make it to practice on time today, or else coach is going to be pissed," Abel announces, making a gesture to the assholes holding me. They step forward, and the next thing I know, I'm falling onto the tiled floor. My head hits and pain ricochets through my body. A scream works its way up my throat, which causes them to laugh harder as they exit the bathroom, leaving me lying there in a puddle of water.

I lie on the cold floor, my tears mixing with the liquid beneath me. Then and there, I vow to leave this god-awful town and never look back. Hopefully, I can get Dad to go with me.

Not wanting to be caught in my current situation, I move up onto my knees and slowly stand. The room begins to spin and I reach out, holding on to the bathroom stall, trying to stop the bile that's working its way up. My head is pounding and everything hurts, but I know I can't stay here. I still need to get to the classroom for my things.

Stumbling out of the bathroom, my vision blurs and I end up falling to the floor in the hallway, barely catching myself from hitting face first.

"Are you okay, Dominic?" a faint familiar voice rings out.

"Huh?" I try to stand, but lose my balance and fall again.

"Shit, they did it again? Come on, let me help you up and get you out of this hallway before the bell rings." With her help, I'm able to get on my feet. She

puts my arm over her shoulder and wraps hers around my waist. We stay close to the wall of lockers, so I can hold on to it for support. "I'm going to sit you down inside of the janitor's closet until the hallway clears. If these assholes see you like this, they'll just lay into you some more."

"I need to get my books," I gasp, stopping for a second time to catch my breath.

"Where are they? I'll get them."

"Mr. Grayson's Literature class, room 304," I answer softly through my bruised lips. Any resistance I would normally have to her retrieving them is gone.

"Okay, we're here." She opens the door and helps me inside, turning on the light. The brightness immediately makes me wince. "Sorry," she says, and I try to focus on the familiar voice, my vision clearing a little as I look at her.

She's blonde and wearing clothes that are far bigger than she needs. As she looks at me, I see nothing but kindness shining back in her eyes. I know she's been in a couple of my classes, but she's always quiet and keeps to herself, much like me. "I'll be right back. Don't try to leave," she tells me as she pokes her head out of the door, looking both ways before disappearing out of it. The shrill of the bell echoes through the cramped room just after she leaves, causing my head to pound even more. It feels like a grenade going off inside of it.

As I wait, I slowly start to feel more like myself. It seems like forever before she returns. Finally, she pokes her head in the door and looks around, spotting me in the corner where I moved, resting my head against the wall. "Good, you're still here. I think I got everything that was yours. Mr. Grayson asked where you were and I told him you were sitting in the office and that Mrs. Penny asked me to come get your stuff because you weren't feeling well."

"Thank you. I'm sorry. I know your face, but I can't remember your name," I say, ashamed of not knowing who my savior today is.

"It's Lorna, and you and I are going to be best friends. Loners like us need to stick together against the Abel's of the world." She winks and flashes me a *smile. Instantly, I know in my heart what she's saying will be true.*

CHAPTER ONE

NIC

Present Day

I startle awake, soaking wet with sweat. Breathing hard, I rub my chest, trying to work out the tightness, and look around. Fuck! Not again. It's been three months since I got that fucking invitation in the mail for my high school reunion. If Chad wasn't sitting right beside me that day, asking what it was, I would've thrown it straight into the trash and never opened it. But he was, and I did. He didn't ask much more about it, letting me come and talk to him when I was ready.

Ever since then, I've been waking up in a panic at least three times a week, reliving a memory from the past. Memories I wanted to keep buried deep down in my psyche.

Sitting up, I pull my knees to my chest and rest my elbows on them. I blow out a deep breath and rake my hands through my hair, trying to pull myself out of the nightmare. I'm not in high school anymore. When I ignored the emails, I thought it would be the end of it. I even went as far to block their fucking address, but no, whoever is heading up this shit show somehow found my address.

Chad moves beside me, just before his large warm hand reaches out, and slips between my chest and legs, pulling me back down in bed. "Baby, this has to stop. You need to rest." His deep, husky voice cracks from sleep. The tone of it completely different from the dominant one he uses that always sends me teetering over the edge, ready to comply like an obedient submissive.

"I know. During the day I do well pushing it to the back, but at night, it all comes rushing to the forefront." I sigh, rolling into him, letting my arm drape over his muscular, tattooed chest.

"Baby boy, let Daddy help you relax so you can sleep." His tone instantly changes, more controlling and silky, making my body come to life. I'm ready for whatever my master has in mind, knowing he will comfort me when I need it most.

When he rolls away from me, I take in the muscular ripples of his back, and my cock stirs in response. I hear him open his bedside table, or as I like to call it, the drawer of wonders. He turns back to me with some lube and an anal vibe wand, with little beads going down the length of it. It's my favorite.

"You look delicious, baby boy, lying there, waiting so patiently for me." He sits up, letting the sheet drop around his waist. "Hands up," he commands, and I eagerly obey. He takes hold of them and winds the satin cuffs connected to our bed around each, locking my arms firmly in place above my head.

"What's your word, baby boy?"

"Tamale." My voice comes out husky and full of need. And with one look from him, I turn into his needy little slut. The look I know so well. One that promises both pleasure and pain to help me get out of my head.

"Good." He trails the tips of his fingers down my chest, goosebumps prickling my skin as his touch sets me on fire.

Chad stops just short of my hard cock and rips the sheet off my body, exposing my naked body to him. "My baby boy is eager for me, I see." Opening the lube, he squeezes some into his hand and spreads it along the length of the wand. I moan loudly as I watch his hands move up and down it, the action turning me on even more.

"You're going to take this while I play, and no coming. Do you understand?" I nod, but that's not good enough and I know it. "My boy is being naughty; he knows he must use his words."

"Yes, Daddy, I understand." I gasp at the sting of the leather crop as he slaps it across my thighs. *Where the hell did he have that hidden?*

"Now my baby boy needs to obey, especially if he wants to come for Daddy."

Spreading my legs, he traces his fingers around my asshole. Slipping just the tip of one if them in and out, teasing me, and I tense involuntarily. The tight ring of muscles resists at first, but I relax, taking a deep breath and blowing it out, allowing his whole finger to slip inside. I moan again, desperate for more. "Such a responsive boy. My cock loves filling your hole. It's my second favorite opening of yours to fill."

He pumps his finger in and out, adding another as he scissors them, preparing my tight hole for what's to come. Fuck if he knows how to make me feel good, to forget all my worries. Then, suddenly, his hands are gone. The loss of his touch leaves me feeling empty. "Baby boy, what's your color?"

"Green," I cry out, trying not to squirm. Chad is so good about using our color system constantly checking in to see where I'm at; to make sure I'm still present and willing in all he does. Green is good, yellow means I'm okay and keep going, just slow down, and red is stop. The last color I've never had to use.

"Good," he praises, running his hand up my thigh. A second later, something enters my ass and a buzzing sound rings out in the room. The vibration immediately makes me arch my back, almost sending me over the edge. "That's it baby boy, take it all, but you better not fucking come, not until I say you can," he growls.

My eyes focus on him as he moves his body between my legs. He picks up the catclaw pinwheel and slips it on his finger, glancing up. His eyes lock on mine and he smirks. My daddy kept some of the goodies he chose earlier a secret, placing them just out of my sight until he needed them. The prickling sensation continues as he runs it up my leg, stopping just at the apex of my thigh. When he licks up the length of my shaft, it surprises me and I about come right then and there.

"Daddy," I cry out, the sensations overwhelming.

"Yes, baby boy." His tone is husky and deep; everything a leading man in an erotic dream would sound like. Before I can respond, he runs the pinwheel up my other leg.

"I need to come. Please?" I beg, gasping as the vibrations of the wand dance along my prostate, teetering me so close to the edge, my balls draw up.

His hand disappears between my legs before I feel the wand begin to thrust in and out of my ass. His mouth slides down on my cock ever so slowly as I stay perfectly still; even though all I want to do is buck upward, fucking his face until I shoot my load down his throat. But I don't. Punishment for doing that would be an orgasm denial.

"Ahhh—aaa—Daaddddyyy." I struggle in my restraints as Chad bobs up and down. I feel my control slipping when the warmth of his mouth is added to the vibrations of the wand. Sweat breaks out all over my body as I fight to hold back my release. "I can't hold it. Pllleease, Daddy, I need to come."

Chad raises off my dick with a loud pop and looks at me, drool hanging off his chin. "My sweet baby boy, I know you do. I'm going to put my mouth back on your fat cock and you're gonna come in my mouth, giving me everything. But not until then. Do you understand?"

"Yes, Daddy."

Chad teases me, licking up and down the length of my shaft. Each time I think he's about to sink down onto my painfully hardened length, he doesn't. He reaches out, taking my balls into his hand, kneading them roughly. "Time to come, baby boy."

His lips open wide, swallowing my cock, and he sucks on me like a man starved while massaging my balls. Moments later, my back arches up, and my release explodes out of me. Stars dance along the back of my eyes as I shoot my load down his throat, groaning.

Chad licks his lip, catching anything that may have escaped. The vibrations of the wand stop as it's pulled from me. My body feels like jelly and I can't move a muscle. I watch as he sits up, picking up the toy and lube and placing them on the dresser to clean later. Only then does he reach up and free my hands. He checks each of my wrists, making sure they're okay before returning to his spot in bed. Pulling me close, he wraps his arms around me and I rest my head on his chest, listening to his thunderous heartbeat. He strokes his hands along my back, whispering soothing words until I drift off to sleep.

I'm tired as shit this morning, but I have to head into the office to meet with the architect about the designs for our newest club, The Dungeon. This is our second run through, and if they don't have acceptable plans this time, Chad and I plan to fire them. They think just because they came recommended to us, they can dick us around to get more money. What they don't know is that Chad and I have done our research, and this isn't our first time. We've had five **BDSM** clubs built in various cities over the last two years. We know what we want and we won't settle or be manipulated into anything else. As Chad so eloquently put it, 'the only person who will be manhandling anyone is me', and fuck if I don't want him doing it to me.

Stepping into my office, Jesselyn scurries behind, right on my heels, ready to give me all the updates for the day. She drones on and on, and all I can think about is that I've got time scheduled later this week for one of our new movies. Running Sanmat Corporation is mentally exhausting, and performing helps maintain my sanity. Chad and I both love the thrill of performing in porn, especially since it made us who we are today and brought us together.

"Also, I blocked your schedule next month for your reunion. Will I need to make any travel arrangements for you?" The mention of school pulls me from my thoughts and back to the present.

"No, I'll handle those. We're done here. Please let me know when Mr. Jackson arrives."

"Yes, sir." She stands, taking a moment to smooth down her pencil skirt before walking out of the room and shutting the door behind her.

Leaning back in my captain's chair, I let out a sigh. This fucking reunion is going to be the death of me. Standing up, I walk over to the wet bar, pouring a glass of whiskey, and sip it slowly. I need to keep my wits about me for this meeting, but thinking about the reunion is driving me insane. *Why did I ever agree to go to this thing?*

One simple answer, Lorna. If it wasn't for her, I wouldn't be going. Well, that's not entirely true; there's also the off chance that Carla will be there. She and Lorna were the only bright lights in that whole fucking school.

Moving back over to my desk, I sit down and turn on my laptop. I bite the bullet and book two first-class seats. Might as well get this over with. Next up, finding a place to stay. I look up the number for The Manor of Brighton Hill. Dialing the number, the phone rings three times before someone picks up.

Gladys, who answers, is so sweet as she handles reserving a room for Chad and me with a king-size bed. After hearing my last name, she is quick to apologize for my father's death, going on and on about what a wonderful man he was. My father's death was a tragedy, one that still rattles me, especially with all the secrets his death exposed. Saying goodbye, I hang up and blow out a deep breath. I scrub my hand down my face, thankful that's over with.

A knock at the door pulls my attention. "Come in," I call out.

"Mr. Santini, Mr. Jackson is here and waiting in the conference room."

"Thank you, Jesselyn. I'll be right there."

Standing, I take one last sip of the whiskey before heading to my meeting, praying like hell they have their shit together this time.

CHAPTER TWO

NIC

Walking in the door, I drop my keys in the bowl that sits on top of the desk and place my laptop bag on the floor.

"Chad, are you home?" I call out. I didn't see his car in the drive, but I was too lazy to pull my car into the garage, so it's possible he's home.

"In the kitchen," he calls back.

Reaching up, I undo my tie as I head toward his voice, pulling it over my head and stuffing it in my pocket. Stepping inside, I see Chad standing at the granite counter, pulling takeout containers with the name Angelino's on them from a bag. Our favorite Italian restaurant. "Thought we'd vegetate on the couch tonight and continue watching Bridgerton."

Stepping around the counter, I kiss him on the cheek. This man is the love of my life and was my savior in one of my darkest times.

"I made the hotel reservations and booked our plane tickets today," I blurt out, glancing at him out of the corner of my eye as I open the fridge and pull out a bottle of water.

"So, does that mean you're positive about going? You know if you don't, it's okay too. From what you told me, that school owes you nothing but an apology."

"No, I promised Lorna I'd go. Plus, it gives me a chance to visit Dad. I haven't seen him since his funeral and I didn't really see anyone or do anything in town."

"Why don't you go change and meet me in the living room?" He gives me a stern look, letting me know this is not a request.

Setting the bottle of water on the counter, I head upstairs. As I step into our room, I take off my jacket and kick off my shoes. Laying the jacket over the chaise lounge, I finish taking off the rest of my clothes, putting them with the jacket. Glancing back at them, a memory takes over.

"Baby boy, is this how we treat our clothes?" he asks sternly.

"No, Daddy, but I didn't feel like putting them away," I whine. "I've had a long day, and putting clothes away was the least of my worries."

"What happens to bad little boys who disobey?" His voice is commanding, hitting me right in my core, and my cock twitches.

"They get punished," I answer.

"That's right. Now strip, baby boy, and get on the bench." He steps out of the room, and I immediately do as he says.

I stay there in position on the bench, my hard cock hanging in the wind as my ass is stuck up in the air. The door shuts behind me and I know Daddy has returned. "Good boy," he praises, filling me with warmth.

He stops in front of me, fastening the straps around my wrists before stepping behind me. His fingertips trail over my exposed ass cheeks, electricity dancing along my skin at his touch. His hands brush along my legs as he fastens the straps around my ankles.

"Now, be a good boy and just maybe I'll let you come at the end," his voice hitting my ears like velvet. He smooths his hand over my ass, slipping his fingers down the length of my crack. When he reaches my tight hole, he rubs light circles around the rim and I moan, my body jerking from the pleasure coursing through it.

"No, now, none of that, baby boy." His touch disappears, before his hands reappear, sliding something on my dick. I instantly recognize it as a cock ring. A buzzing noise rings out through the quietness of the room, as a warm liquid drips along my hole, just before something is pushed inside of it.

"Fuck!" My body arches as the sensations hit me all at once.

"Shhh, baby boy, you didn't get permission to scream. Now, no coming, remember that." His gruff voice soothes me as light feathery touches dance along my spine. "Next time, my baby boy will put his clothes where they belong."

My cock hardens at the memory and I debate whether I may want to replay that night or not. It ended in the best reward he's ever given me for being so good. My brattiness and the need to be punished wins out. Smirking, I pick up the clothes and drop them on the floor before pulling some gray sweats and a shirt out of my dresser. Let's see what he has to say about that.

Headed back downstairs, I take the stairs at a run, and jump from the last to the floor. My little memory fueling me with energy. Chad is sitting down on the couch, the food set out on the coffee table in front of us, and two glasses of wine waiting.

"How was your day?" He looks at me, picking up a glass and handing it to me. I can see the sympathy in his eyes, knowing how I've been feeling about this reunion.

"It was long, but okay. I think the architect has finally gotten his shit together. The plans looked good today, so I approved them and they're being sent to the construction foreman." I raise the wine to my lips, taking a sip.

"Well, that's a relief. I was dreading the thought of having to interview new ones," he says, tapping his finger on my plate, letting me know I need to eat.

"Me too, but thankfully we don't have to worry about it. Also, just a reminder, we're due on set Wednesday at three for filming. Janetta is going to be doing the scene with us." I pick up my fork, taking a bite of lasagna. Moaning as the first taste of the delicious, cheesy goodness touches my tongue.

"I like her, not to mention she has an amazing rack. It's only gotten better since she delivered her baby. Is she still breastfeeding?" Chad asks, reaching over to swipe a bit of cheese off my chin.

"Yeah, I think she is. But I personally think her pussy is better. She tastes delicious when she squirts."

"Keep talking like that and I'm going to have you bent over this couch, pounding my cock inside that tight ass of yours." He crashes his lips on mine, capturing my cries, as his hand cups my cock through my pants.

"Don't tempt me, Daddy," I moan breathlessly after he releases my lips.

He picks up and his fork and glances at me, smirking, with a look in his eyes, promising pleasure. When he looks back at his plate and starts eating, I don't move. I just soak him in, reflecting on how lucky I am. A few seconds later, he must notice I'm not eating.

"Now eat up," he orders sternly. We turn the television on, picking up our show right where we left off. We spend the next hour eating and bantering back and forth about what's happening on the screen.

Not able to eat another bite, I place my fork on the plate and stand, picking up both mine and his, taking them to the kitchen. Once I've scraped off any leftover food into the trash, rinsed them and placed them in the dishwasher for later, I head back to the living room. Shocked to see Chad sitting there, with my senior yearbook on his lap, flipping through the pages. Instantly, I'm on alert.

"What are you doing with that?" I ask, my voice raised. It comes out sharper than I meant for it to.

"With us going to the reunion, I thought you could tell me about some of the people you went to school with. Share some memories with me. I know those weren't good times for you, but you can't keep them squashed away. They will fester and eat away at your soul. Now sit down beside me and I may forget the tone that was just in your voice." He glares at me, eyebrow cocked, waiting to see if I disobey.

I stand there for a moment, hating that he's right. My feelings about high school are what's keeping me up at night, unable to sleep, as memories pour back into my mind. Finally, I relent and take a seat beside him, pulling half the book onto my lap.

"For you, high school was amazing, but for me, it was hell. Every day I spent there was fucking torture. Lorna and Carla were the only bright spots," I start.

"Carla, she was the girl you pined over? Your chemistry partner, right?"

"Yeah, she was in homeroom with me since eighth grade when she moved to town, and when we hit high school, she was my lab partner every year for science." I smile, remembering her sweet smile and her kind words when she spoke to me.

"Did you two ever date?"

"No, she was out of my league and she never looked at me like that. She was always nice to me, even apologized for her friends."

"Maybe you can reconnect with her." He gazes at me, lust in his eyes, and I know what he's thinking.

"I have you, Chad. Who else do I need?" I lean over, kissing him, taking his hand in mine.

"Nic, we've known from the beginning we always wanted to bring in a third, a female. You've loved this girl since high school, so if she's available, then why not?"

"You've never met her. What if you don't like her? She may not even be into our lifestyle," I remind him. Hell, I don't know if she even knew I was bisexual.

"If you like her, I will. Besides, we're getting older and eventually we'll want kids. As for the lifestyle, we can ease her into it."

I cut my eyes at him, but he's not even paying attention to me.

"Chad—" I start, but he places his fingers over my lips.

"No, I'm not a fool, Nic. I've heard you talk about her over the years, how your eyes light up when you do. That's not how you are with someone who was a passing crush. She meant more to you, and I'm okay with that. While a first love is one that sticks with you forever and even harder when you never truly had them, I'm your last love and will be with you till your dying day. I'm willing to share you, to share her, be Daddy to you both. I want our family complete and one day I want someone calling me Daddy for a whole different reason; a child."

"Chad..." I pause, trying to find the right words. Emotional over what he's saying. "You are far more than my last love. You are the greatest love of my life. Let's not worry so much about it. For all I know, she is happily married, with kids, and doesn't remember who I am. But—"

"I do love a good but." He smirks, waggling his eyebrows.

Laughter flows out of me. Chad has this amazing gift for lightening the mood and I love him for it. "Like

I was saying, but if you want to meet her, broach her, feel out the situation, I will make it happen for you."

"Now, tell me some more about Brighton, who these people are." He flips the page and laughs.

"Oh my god, is that Lorna?" He slams his hand down on the book, pointing at her picture.

"Yeah. That's my bestie."

"Man, she's beautiful, don't get me wrong. But damn, she had a glow up, from baggy clothes where you can't tell she had a figure, to a hot as fuck, blue hair, tatted, pouty lip goddess. Did she have it as bad as you?" he asks, as he flips the page.

"We were both bullied. Honestly, I don't know how to compare it, but we did have a common tormenter throughout high school." I flip the pages until I find a picture of him, landing on the hockey team and point. "Abel Burakoff, the god of hockey if you asked anyone at Brighton. He was an utter asshole if you asked me or Lorna. He's one of the main reasons she's going to this thing. She has some type of revenge plot in place."

"So you both have reasons; you want to reunite with the girl you desired and Lorna will probably want to blow his whole act up in smoke." Chad has always been so eloquent with his words.

We continue flipping through the book for the next hour, as I tell him who everyone is. The longer we sit there, the sleepier I get. I try my hardest to stifle a yawn, but it doesn't go unnoticed.

"Come on baby boy, let Daddy put you to bed." He closes the yearbook, sitting it back on the table, before picking up the remote and turning off the television. Taking my hand in his, he guides me up the stairs, where he is sure to notice my bratty deviance from earlier. I somehow don't think I'll be going to bed early and I'm okay with that.

CHAPTER THREE

NIC

Three Months Ago

"Lorna, this isn't the best time. I'm at work." I grunt out, trying to hold a groan in.

"So, when has it bothered you before when I interrupted you at work? Oh, wait, are you — no fucking way. What are you doing? You're talking so you can't be the giver, so you have to be the receiver. Is it a guy? Girl? What does the person look like?" she rambles out the onslaught of questions instead of getting to the damn point of why she called.

"It's a guy. Newbie, we're just practicing before we redo the scene," I hiss out as the guy peers up at me with puppy dog eyes, seeking approval for how well he's sucking my cock. In my home life I'm the submissive, but here on set, I'm the dominant one, unless I'm filming with Chad. "Hold on one sec, Lorna," I tell her before looking down at the man. "Just like that, Jason, but take your time. It's not a race. All the way to the back of your throat. While you're doing it, you can alternate between massaging my balls and letting your fingers grip my ass, teasing my asshole."

Just like an eager little puppy, he follows my directions, and fuck if he's not a quick learner. Especially for someone who has never been with a man before. Hence the reason for the practice run, we need it to look natural, not forced, on his end. My moan slips past my lips, floating through the line to Lorna, who lets out her own little whimper.

"Lorna, are you playing with yourself to the sounds of my blowjob?"

"What if I am? It wouldn't be the first time. Now, back to why I called. Did you get the invite and please tell me you're going?"

"Ahh ffffuu " I moan out, because damn if this dude isn't doing a great job. "I'm not going, Lorna. You know high school was fucking hell for me. Why would I want to go back and see any of those assholes?"

"For me, Dominic. Please. I want to go back and exact some revenge on Abel. He needs to pay for how he treated us."

"Do you really think he cares what he did to you? To me? He's probably still the jerk he was in school," I remind her.

"I don't care. Please, just say you'll go for me. Don't make me pull the best friend card," What she's saying doesn't match with how she sounds, her voice husky and needy through the phone.

"Fine, I'll think about it. I need to go. Talk to you later." I tell her before ending the call, not giving her a chance to reply.

Reaching down, I slide my fingers through Jason's midnight black locks, winding his hair around my hands. Gripping it tightly, I thrust forward, pushing my hard shaft further down his throat. I can feel him gagging on the size. "Relax your mouth and it will be easier. Believe it or not, you'll encounter men with larger cocks than me." He mumbles incoherently around my dick, but I keep going. The need to have a release overriding everything else at the moment.

I feel his hand on my neck, before his breath dances along the shell of my ear and I shiver. "You're teaching him so well, baby boy. Such a good teacher." He praises me and instantly I'm shooting ropes of hot cum down Jason's throat as he swallows every drop.

I keep my hand on Jason's head, holding him there for a second more while I catch my breath. Pulling my cock out of his mouth, drool dribbles everywhere. "Get up. You did a good job and will do well when they start filming. Chad, this is our new employee."

Chad sits down beside me, placing his left hand on my shoulder before reaching out with his right, taking Jason's in his and helping him to stand. Pulling him closer, he crashes his lips on his, forcing his tongue into Jason's mouth, kissing him deeply before pulling away. "Nice to meet you, Jason. My partner tastes amazing on your lips."

The guy starts to stutter, no doubt falling victim to all that Chad is. I can't blame him; I find Chad irresistible as well. "You're free to go, Jason, don't mind him. Go get something to eat and get cleaned up. They'll be filming your scene with Carlos in an hour. Just do as amazing with him as you did with me." I give him a supportive smile, leaning into Chad.

"Yes, sir," Jason says before turning and rushing off.

"You always do so good working with the new hires. Now that you're relaxed, do you want to grab something to eat?"

"Yeah, I'm starving. How's Chinese?" I pull away from him, picking up my clothing from the chair and dressing.

"Sounds perfect. Did Lorna get a hold of you? She called the house this morning and was looking for you, going on about some guy she wanted to destroy and needing to talk to you."

"She got ahold of me. Actually, during the blow job you walked in on," I tell him, hoping he will just drop it and leave it at that.

"What was she talking about?" he pries. Fuck, I hate reliving high school.

"You know we went to school together. Well, it's our ten-year reunion coming up and, well, you saw the invitation." We take off walking hand in hand.

"That's right, I had mine two years ago. It was a blast, you know, you went with me. I almost forgot you got that invitation." He opens the door, leading us to the elevator that goes to the parking garage for employees.

"Yeah, but you were popular. I wasn't. You weren't bullied, while I was, every day. Anyway, we had a bully in common and she wants to exact some revenge and wants me to go with her."

"You should. Show all of them how much you've changed, how successful you are and rub it in their faces. Plus, you have me on your arm. Just think about it. I'll be with you and who knows, you may have fun and get the closure you need." We step up to our charcoal gray Audi R8, and he opens the passenger door for me.

"I don't know, but I'll think about it." There's a gnawing sensation in the pit of my stomach just thinking about going back to that hellhole. However, it would be nice to rub how much money I have in their faces, and how great my life is with Chad. A glimpse of the blonde beauty I crushed over all through high school slips into my mind, Carla. I wonder if she'll be there. Is she married? Does she have kids? Hell, does she remember me or think about me?

Chad starts the car up, revving the engine for fun, before shifting the car into gear and backing out of the spot.

CHAPTER FOUR

CARLA

"Order up!" Sal shouts from the kitchen. Heading to the food counter, I pick up my order before delivering it to the truck driver at table six. I've been working at the diner off the highway for the last seven years. It was the perfect job, close to the apartment I live in and not directly in town, so I don't have to see the people I went to highschool with that still live here.

"Hey girl," Martha steps up beside me, giving me a hip bump. "Two weeks until the reunion. Are you ready for it?" She has been a godsend since I returned. Not only did she take me and Brandon in until we could get a place of our own, but she helps watch him when I need a break.

"No, and I'm having second thoughts about going. There's no one I want to see, and I really don't want to run into Jack. It's bad enough the shit he spread about me when we broke up." Lifting my hand, I rub my forehead, a headache already forming like it always does when I think about him.

"No, ma'am, you are going. I'm watching that sweet boy of yours for the weekend and you are going to have a good time." She places her hands on her hips, stomping her foot at me.

"I only need you to watch him one night and that's only if I go," I remind her.

"No. First, you are going, even if I have to take you there myself. Second, it's three days, so yes, I have him for the weekend."

"Martha, the whole theme is, *who are they now?* I really don't want to show up and only be a waitress, barely making it, living paycheck to paycheck, with my tips being the only reason I keep my power on. And what if Jack is there?"

"There is nothing wrong with being a waitress and an amazing mother. Now, how are you going to handle it if both Jack and Dominic are there?"

"I doubt Dominic will come; he hasn't been back to Brighton since his father died. And besides, Jack doesn't know who Brandon's father really is. I never told him, and he never asked to see the birth certificate." One of the few smart things I did was to lie to Jack about him not being the father, telling him I cheated and was pregnant with someone else's baby. He was so dumb, he never questioned it. Once he heard the baby wasn't his, he ran, never wanting to be a father, and it got me out of an abusive and controlling relationship.

"Hey ladies, this ain't no hen coop, so stop squawking and get back to work. I just saw the bus pull up in front and this place is gonna be swamped in a moment," Sal barks out before giving Martha a wink. One day, he better wise up and ask her out. She won't be single long with how amazing she is.

"Have we ever not handled a crowd?" she snipes at him. He's acting like the two of us can't handle a restaurant full of people, but he knows better. We've done it many times before.

"Come on, Carla, let's get ready for the rush. Don't forget that you and Brandon are coming for dinner tonight. I picked him up something and I can't wait to give it to him," she tells me, smiling as she pulls a stack of menus from underneath the counter and sets them on top of it.

"You've got to stop spoiling him," I whine.

"No, I don't. It's my one joy in life. That boy is special and deserves some goodness in his life." She turns, looking me dead in the eyes. "And you deserve happiness, too. Your life is hard and you're doing it alone and doing an amazing job, but you deserve love. And what if by some slim chance the boy you had a crush on in school shows up? Maybe he felt the same way and still does."

"I don't know. What if he's mad because I never said anything? Is it wrong that I didn't want to be picked on if I went out with him? That when one of the cool kids noticed me and wanted to date me, I jumped on it, even though I still harbored those secret feelings for him?"

"Oh my, Carla. You worry too much. You were a teenager, a kid. No one can blame you for the choices you made back then. Peer pressure is a beast and one we all fall prey to." Right then, the front door opens and a busload of customers make their way in, filling up the empty seats, cutting our conversation short. She looks at me smiling, and we get to work.

Four PM came quickly, and I rushed to pick Brandon up from his after-school program. Thankfully, my old beat up Corolla cranked on the first try. Traffic was a bitch, but I managed to make it in thirty minutes. Stepping inside, I smile at the receptionist before heading down to Brandon's classroom.

Stopping in front of his classroom door, I peek inside, seeing him and a couple other kids sitting at a table playing a board game. He has a huge smile on his face as he laughs along with the other kids about something. Opening the door, I step inside waving to his teacher as I do so. She immediately heads my way.

"Mrs. Sanderson, so good to see you. Brandon finished all of his homework upon arriving today," she announces, making sure I'm aware. "He's been very good today and is such a joy to have."

"Thank you, Mrs. Davis. He enjoys coming here after school. I'll just get him and we'll be on our way." She nods her head as I walk over to him.

"Mom!" he screams out. "Can I have just five more minutes? We're almost done and I'm winning." His sweet little voice, so bubbly, warms my heart.

"Five minutes, then we have to go. Besides, we're having dinner with Martha tonight and she told me she has something for you."

I step away, moving over to his cubbie to get his jacket and backpack as a couple of mothers enter the room, both of which I went to high school with. Their voices carry, though I doubt they were trying to be quiet. *"Can you believe it? I heard she replied back that she was going to the reunion,"* one says, before the brunette pipes up. *"Jack is going to be there, too. I still can't believe she cheated on someone as good as he was to her. And he's still covering for her, not saying who the real father of her child is. I still can't believe she tried to pawn him off as his."*

I give them a wave, prompting their fake smiles. *Fucking cunts.* More than ever, I want to move away from this town, where the man who beat the shit out of me behind closed doors is portrayed as the victim, while I'm the villain of the story.

"Brandon, come on baby, time to go," I call out to him, as he stands from the table and rushes over after saying goodbye to his friends.

"Mommy, can we get ice cream on the way home?"

God, I want so much to tell him yes, but I can't. All the money I made today in tips has to go toward the rent. I'm already late, and what I made will just cover the remaining balance. "Not today, sweetie," I tell him, as I watch his face drop.

We head out to the car, and I try to keep him distracted from his disappointment by asking about his day and reminding him about the surprise that Martha has for him tonight. Once we're home, I send him upstairs while I drop the envelope with the rent into the building supervisor's mailbox. Thankful that I didn't have to see him. The stench of beer and cigarette smoke wafting off of him, and the way he leers at me, makes my stomach turn and twist in knots.

Making sure it goes all the way in the slot, I turn and rush up the stairs, just in case he should hear me in the hallway. Brandon is standing just outside the door, leaning against the wall as he kicks his foot back and forth, making a scuffing sound. He looks up at me before asking me the question I've been dreading, the one I keep dancing around answering for him.

"Mommy, where's my daddy? All the other kids have daddies. Some live with them and some don't, but they know who he is. Who's mine? Is he mad at me? Does he not like me? Is that why he doesn't come see me?" he asks, with a little frown on his face.

I drop to my knees in front of him, my heart breaking. "Oh baby, your dad is an amazing man and I promise one day he will come for you. Just be patient."

"What's his name? Is it the same as mine, like my friend RJ?"

"No sweetie, his name is Dominic. Now, let's go inside and get cleaned up before going to Martha's for dinner." My answer seems to appease him, as I slowly stand, opening the door, letting him step inside. He takes off running to his bedroom, no doubt ready to play some more while he can. Fuck, I need a drink!

CHAPTER FIVE

NIC

Three Days Before The Reunion

Pulling my suitcase out of the closet and dropping it on the bed, I let out a deep sigh. My stomach twists tighter into knots the closer the day of our flight gets. Thankfully, we're flying into the larger airport in San Francisco and renting a car to drive into Brighton. Chad has continually given me reassurance that when I'm ready to leave, we're out of there. Lorna, on the other hand, has threatened me with bodily harm if I cut out early.

Sliding the hangers along the rack, I stop on my black Versace studded Barocco silhouette blazer with matching pants for Saturday night's event. I know Chad plans to wear his charcoal gray suit. The one that reminds me of that Christian Grey guy from those books women were drooling over, and not from the lips on their faces.

Moving over to the bed, I lay it flat, planning to place it in Chad's garment bag to keep from wrinkling it. Stepping back into the closet, I sift through the clothing, pulling out some jeans, dressier shirts, and t-shirts. Taking each of them off the hanger, I fold and place them in the suitcase, trying to leave room for Chad's clothes. Hopefully, we won't need another one.

Last thing to go in are dress shoes, socks, boxers and I'm done. Chad and I usually sleep in the nude, so no need to pack pajamas. Once I've got everything, I sit down on the bed and pull out my phone to run through my checklist for traveling, making sure everything is in order. I may be slightly OCD, needing everything to be in its place and not wanting to forget something important. Once I'm confident I have everything done, I pick up my phone, scrolling through my contacts until I find the one I'm looking for and send a text.

Me: Have I told you how much I hate you today for making me go to this reunion?

I don't expect her to respond, but I want her to know, anyway.

Lorna: Psshhh, you know you love my ass. Besides, don't think I don't know you're hoping Carla's coming. BTW, a little birdie told me they got her RSVP that she'd be there.

Me: And who would this birdie be? Are they reliable? Or is this more of your BS to keep me from backing out?

Lorna: It's true. She'll be there. Also, in case you were wondering, she still lives in Brighton. Now shut the hell up, pack, and let's get ready to have some fun and show those fuckers how well we turned out. Guarantee you, they'll be regretting bullying us in school.

Me: I don't care what those fuckers think. In and out. That's my plan, and well, lots of alcohol to get through the weekend.

Lorna: Count me in. Drinks on Friday after the meet and greet. Heard there's a new trashy dive bar with loud music and a dance floor. I think it's called the Eagles Nest.

Me: Sounds good. Also, did you hear that Olivia is dating that jerk Rhett from school?

Lorna: No!!!!!!!!! You're fucking with me. There's no way. Has he drugged her? Threatened her with some type of sex tape or something? What could she see in him?

"Hey babe, where are you?" Chad shouts from downstairs.

"In the bedroom," I quickly respond, looking around the room, ensuring everything is tidy. If it isn't, I'll be punished. Win-win for me, since I like a little pain with my pleasure.

Me: Don't know. GTG Daddy is home.

Lorna: DDDDDAAAAADDDDYYYYYY!!!!!!

I can't with this girl. She's the only one I talk to about the explicit details of our sex life. Only because she'd never spill the beans and, well, it's just way too hot to keep to myself. Obviously, Chad had to give me permission first. *That was a fun night.*

Chad steps inside the room and I can't help but notice how his eyes sweep around the room, landing on the suitcase on the bed. A grin crosses his face, a definite sign of approval.

"Save some room for my clothes in there?" He nods his head, gesturing toward the luggage.

"Yes, I even pulled out your suit so I can put it with mine in the garment bag. Figured I'd leave the rest of your clothes for you to pack."

He gets a sly look in his eyes and smirks. "Pack any toys?"

Shaking my head, he lets out a laugh. "That's okay, I'll pack some. Even add in a few that maybe Carla will like."

"Chad, we—"

"I know, but it doesn't hurt to be prepared."

"Chad, she may not accept," I gesture between the two of us. "First, I wasn't out in high school. Not to mention she may not, as I voiced to you before very adamantly, be into the lifestyle we are. Are you ready to lead a vanilla life if she is okay with the two of us?"

He stands there for a minute, his brows furrowing as he thinks. "If she is who you want, and she's okay with being with the two of us, then yes, I can. For my non-vanilla, I still have you and our movies. I'll be okay." He crosses the room, moving the suitcase before sitting down beside me, angling his body to mine and taking my hand in his. "The only thing I want in this life is you, for you to be happy, and one day, a kid. Everything else is just frosting on the cake. Believe it or not, I was once a vanilla kind of guy." We both gaze into each other's eyes, like we're in a standoff before we burst out into laughter.

"Seriously though, I think it's more facing everyone that treated me like shit in school. There's nothing we have in common and there's no way in hell I'm going to pretend to be nice to them, like the past never happened."

"I don't expect you to, Nic. But maybe this is the closure you need to let those things from the past stay there. A memory, nothing more, that can fade from your mind until it's just a blip on the radar. Then who knows, maybe Carla will give us a chance.You get the lost love. I get someone new, and the chance at kids." Fuck, the way he looks at me with those beautiful emerald eyes, the same color as our comforter. There was a reason I picked that shade. It reminded me of him.

"Maybe. Who's to say she is still single or even interested in me? I mean, she wasn't in school. Then she started dating that dick, Jack. Hell, she only really started talking to me in ninth grade, since we were lab partners. Prior to that, she sat in front of me in homeroom, but she never talked to me. Instead, Carla was always in the middle of a conversation with the other girls who sat around her."

"Tell me about the first time you talked to her." He slides off his shoes, scooting back on the bed, resting against the headboard before pulling my body into his. He wraps his arm around my shoulder, allowing me to rest my head on his chest.

Taking a deep breath, I let my mind dance backward, to that first day of ninth grade in physical science. The teacher had a note written on the chalkboard that seats would be assigned by alphabetical order, and for no reason would they be changed. As we came in, we were to check with her for our seating assignment. My heart sank, thinking about who my lab partner could be.

"Dominic, you are at the third table on the left. Please take the left seat," Mrs. Pinkerton instructs me. Slowly walking to the back, I barely miss tripping over Rhett's extended leg. He and the guy across from him cackle like hyenas when I stumble, but thankfully, I don't face-plant on the ground. I didn't realize at the time it wouldn't be the worst thing to happen to me.

I quickly scurry to my seat, wanting to sit down before someone tries to pull the stool out from under me or something worse. Once I'm safely seated, I pull out my notebook and textbook and begin flipping through the pages. Anything to distract me from the people sitting and laughing at me.

"Hi, Dominic." The voice is soft and angelic. Wait, is she talking to me? I heard my name. No one talks to me unless they're making fun of me, ever.

"H-h-h-i, Carla." The words stumble out and if she wasn't staring at me with her chocolate eyes, I would slap myself for acting like an utter dork. "You know my name?"

"Duh, we've been in the same homeroom since last year and you sit right behind me. Why wouldn't I know it?" She smiles, and when she does, my dick twitches in my pants, and my heart pounds harder.

"Every day after that, I felt I had a friend. Not one where we hung out at lunch or went to the mall or the movies on weekends. But for one period out of the day, I had someone to talk to." He strokes my shoulders softly as I talk, giving me a little squeeze every once in a while.

"So just stolen moments in science were all you had and for four years, she never knew how you felt?"

"Yep, that's it. For a while she would say hello, then she caught the attention of Jack Hendricks, a junior varsity football player. After that, all our conversations were during class only. So, honestly, I don't think she ever knew." I roll more into his body, tipping my head upward so I can look at him, as I trail circles along his chest with my fingertips.

"Well, she just doesn't know the amazing man she missed out on then. Maybe I should be thankful for that." His chest vibrates underneath me as he laughs.

"Why do you say that?"

"Just that if she started dating you, then she would know how amazing you are and wouldn't have let you go. I may have never met you. You probably wouldn't have done porn when the hot upperclassman mentioned it to you as a way to pay for schooling and then you would've never fallen in love with me."

Lifting up, I crush my lips to his, caressing his tongue with mine. This man is my heart, my soul, my entire being, and I'm so glad I ran into him that day.

"Well, baby boy, guess I should pack."

Sighing, I roll off of him and sit up, giving him the space to sit up and get off the other side of the bed.

"What time is our flight, and when do we get into Brighton?" he asks as he opens his dresser, pulling out some underwear, then a black bag, the one he keeps our toys in, and starts pulling some out of the drawer. I try to sneak a peek, but he turns, his body blocking my view. "Nic!"

"Oh, we have to be at the airport at six AM, so four to check in, and then we land in San Francisco around noon."

"Why are we flying into San Francisco? Isn't there an airport in Brighton? Or at least closer?" He looks at me over his shoulder, confused.

"Just a small one, but I wanted the time to prepare before seeing everyone again. Plus, with the reunion, I wanted to ensure we got a rental car. We can make an adventure out of it. Stop and eat some late lunch at some off the wall restaurant on the highway like we did when we were younger." I try to make my voice sound excited, but I can't hide the anxiety in it. Maybe I should see if I could get some medication to help with it while we're there?

"Okay, sounds like it could be fun." He places the now sealed black bag in the suitcase. I reach for it, but he quickly slaps my hand. "Tsk, tsk, baby boy, no looking until it's time to use them." Laughing, he moves around the bed and heads to the closet, pulling out much of the same types of clothes as I did.

Even though I hate the way I came to meet and get close to Chad, I'm forever thankful I did. I love this man more than life itself.

CHAPTER SIX

CHAD

Thursday June 1st

I know he's anxious about going back to his hometown. Hell, he hasn't been back there in almost eight years. Not since he went to handle his dad's affairs after he died. He was a wreck that day in the library. If I hadn't had to go to the back stack in search of a book for a research project, I never would have heard his silent whimpers. The dominant in me immediately took over, wanting to comfort him, but I had to be cautious with him. I needed to know if he was even into men, if he would be okay with my lifestyle. How I live, what I do.

Over the next month, our friendship grew as well as our attraction, with Nic finally coming out of the closet as being bisexual. It was a liberating moment for him, and it thrilled me to experience it with him. I wasn't sure if he would accept my lifestyle, but after visiting a club with me and taking part in his first scene, he was a natural. Before I knew it, we were making movies together and raking in the money. His fear of having to drop out of college disappeared, his degree making us the financial success we are today.

"Ready, babe?" he calls out from the living room.

The OCD in me is delaying us from leaving. It nagged at me to unplug all the electronics in the house except the fridge. You never know, something could happen, an electrical spark that could cause a fire. It's something my mother always did when we went out of town and it carried over to me. Nic finds it infuriating, since he always forgets and starts cussing at whatever appliance he's trying to use when it doesn't turn on. He knows better than to say anything. Last time he had to go a week with me edging him, not allowing him to orgasm.

"Yeah, just finished." He groans at my response, and I can't help but smile. My hand twitches, ready to smack his ass. Stepping into the living room, I see him already waiting at the door, suitcase, garment and overnight bag on the floor beside him.

"Chad—" he begins, but I hold my hand up, stopping him before he says another word.

"Nope, don't even finish. It's been eight years. You know, there's no sense in griping or acting like it's something new or annoying. You should be used to it by now." Leaning in, I graze his lips with mine softly before reaching down, kissing him softly, taking the handle of the suitcase, and picking up the other two bags. "Let's go."

We step out the door, Nic locking up behind us, and head to the car. After placing our bags in the trunk, I head to the driver's side, and Nic slides into the passenger side.

Turning the car on, I let it run while I sit there, tapping my fingers on the steering wheel. After a few seconds, I blow out a deep breath and shift so that I can face him.

"Nic, we can take the bags out, and cancel all our reservations, screw getting any money back. If this trip is going to cause you anxiety, we don't need to go. I'll handle Lorna. Just say the word baby boy and I'll cut the car off. Otherwise, I'm backing out of the driveway. Either way, I'll be right there at your side, supporting you, being the rock you need if it gets too tough." I wait, giving him the time he needs to make a choice. He's either going to face the ghosts of his past, or let them continue to eat away at him, from the crack in his mind he stores them in.

"As much as I want to say fuck it and go back inside the house and climb back into bed with you, I'm not. Let's do this. I'm going to show all those assholes who I am now."

"That's my boy. Let's go. We got a girl to win over if she's still single." Leaning in closer, I suck his bottom lip between mine before pulling away, teasing him.

He laughs under his breath as he focuses his gaze out the window. We plan to stop at his parent's grave site and put some flowers on it, and make sure it's being taken care of. He doesn't remember his mother, since she died when he was only five from cancer. When we opened our video company and made our first hundred thousand in profit, I'd asked him if he wanted to have his parent's bodies relocated here, to be closer to him and he said no. His father loved Brighton and Nic knew that is where he would want to be.

Reaching out, I grip his knee, giving it a reassuring squeeze as we ride to the airport in silence. One way or another, this will be a trip neither of us will ever forget.

We finally landed in San Francisco. Now on to the next leg of our trip; the two-hour drive to Brighton.

After collecting our luggage, which thankfully arrived safely with us, we head to the bus that will take us to the building to get our rental car. About thirty minutes later, we're walking out of the rental company with the keys to a black Nissan Armada.

"Want to drive us to your old hometown, or should I?" I hold out the keys, waiting for him to decide. When he takes the luggage instead, I have my answer.

We walk side by side to the waiting SUV and load our luggage. Once I'm in the car, I key in the address for the Inn into the GPS and pull out, while Nic fiddles with the radio. I know he's nervous, but I don't want to pressure him, so I decide to get his mind off coming back to his hometown and change the subject.

"So, I can't remember. Do we have a date for the groundbreaking of the new club?"

"No." The annoyance in his voice is evident. "They've promised to give it to me by Monday. If not, I'm going to light a fire under their asses. Next project, their firm doesn't even get contacted about it. I want to go with someone new. If we didn't have so much invested, I would've already cut them loose."

"Then it's settled. If we haven't heard anything by five on Monday, they're gone. I don't care how much money we have invested, we can make it back." The GPS rattles off the upcoming exit I need to take to merge onto the highway and I hit the blinker as I shift over into the turn lane.

"You're not sly either, Chad."

Playing stupid, I gasp in shock. "I don't have a clue what you're talking about?" It's a lie, but not a bad one.

Nic just shakes his head and laughs, causing me to do the same. "I love you, and I know exactly what you're doing. You're distracting me, so I don't think about where we're going."

Every time he tells me he loves me, I get goosebumps. Before I met Nic, I thought I knew what love was. Damn, was I wrong. It wasn't until him that I truly understood what it meant. If he were to ever leave me, I don't think I would ever feel for someone else what I do for him.

His phone buzzes in his lap, which he quickly picks up, looking at the screen and chuckling. He begins to type and I swear his fingers dance across the screen faster than anyone I've ever seen before. One day I'm going to do a test like my mother used to tell me they did in school to see how many words they can type in a minute. He has to be more than fifty or sixty.

He drops the phone back in his lap, glancing over at me with a smirk. "I can't remember if I told you, but apparently tomorrow night we are meeting up with Lorna and Kylo at some dive bar for drinks after the meet and greet. She told me to let you know and I quote, *'there's no getting out of it'.*"

"Well, a drunk Lorna does always give us a good show. Thank god she didn't pick some higher class place." I sigh a bit in relief. She knows us well, especially Nic, and when we go to a bar, we like the hole in the wall places.

The rest of the ride goes smoothly. We talk about our upcoming shoots, the club we're building, and where we want to go for our vacation in a few months. We always go somewhere tropical for an end of the summer blowout, and this year, we haven't settled on where that is yet. Maybe we can figure it out over the course of this weekend.

The exit for Brighton is up ahead, and my stomach begins to growl. The small breakfast I had long gone, and the protein bar I snagged from the vending machine, disappeared along with it.

"I could go for something to eat. You hungry?" I slowly merge as the exit approaches and take it.

"Yeah, I saw a sign back there for a diner. We can hit it up, then head straight to the Inn and check in after, maybe even take a nap." His little wink at the end isn't very subtle. But that's okay. I'm always down for some hot fun with my man.

"Hope the other guests don't make any noise complaints," I joke.

I come to a stop at the end of the off-ramp and look to the right and left for the diner, forgetting to check the billboard for which direction to turn or confirm the name of it. Nic looks both ways before pointing to a building across the street on the left.

"That looks like it."

He's right, it does, and even if it isn't, apparently it's truck driver approved, judging by the three sitting in the parking lot. And I don't care if it is; at this point, I'm starving and could eat a cow if it was standing in front of me. When the light turns green, I make a left turn.

"As long as they have food and some coffee, then it's fine by me. Remember when we used to hit that all-night café after we would come home from the club when we were in college?"

"Man, do I ever. They had the best eggs, hash browns, and coffee so strong, you had to add a shit ton of sugar to be able to drink it."

I look over quickly, seeing his eyes glaze over like they always do when he talks about his favorite hot beverage.

"Well then, Nic, guess we're stopping here." I turn into the parking lot and pull into the newly vacated spot right by the front door. Turning the car off, I reach to open my door. "Let's eat."

As I step around to the passenger side of the car where Nic is standing, I almost grab his hand, but stop myself at the last minute. I'm not sure if he's ready for everyone here to know his sexuality, even if we are on the outskirts of town.

Nic notices the subtle movement and cocks a brow, looking at me in confusion, before sliding his hand in mine and heading for the front door, opening it for me for a change. We're greeted by an older lady. I try to refrain from thinking of her as elderly because looks can be deceiving.

"Would you like a booth or to sit at the counter?" She doesn't even seem phased by seeing two men holding hands.

Looking around, it kind of reminds me of a Waffle House. There's a long counter, each end is lower with a regular chair, while the middle is higher with stools. The only difference is the dining area is larger, with more booths and tables scattered throughout. You're also not able to see the people cooking your food. "Booth please," Nic answers when I don't.

She picks up a couple of menus and some silverware. "Follow me." We fall in line behind her as she leads us to a table and places the menus along with the silverware down. "Your server will be with you in a moment." We slide into the booth across from each other and smile at her.

Picking up the menus, we look them over as we wait on the server to appear. I see the shadow before I hear the voice.

"What can I—Dominic?!" Her voice rises in shock, sounding slightly shrill.

"Carla..." Nic whispers with wide eyes, and fuck if I don't see why he loved her. She's absolutely gorgeous.

CHAPTER SEVEN

CARLA

He immediately stands, wrapping me in a hug. I don't miss the way his hands rub my back, moving dangerously close to my ass. Inhaling deeply, I catch a whiff of his cologne; very outdoorsy with a hint of rain.

He pulls away, smiling brightly as I stare at him, stunned. "I wasn't expecting to see anyone from school yet. How are you, Carla?" He sits back down, placing his hand on top of the other man's, and my heart sinks a little. *Are they together? Is he gay?* "I'm sorry. How rude of me. This is my partner, Chad."

"It's lovely to meet you, Carla. Nic wasn't lying when he said you were beautiful." He reaches out with his free hand and I place mine in it. He holds on to it far longer than he should before releasing me.

"Nice to meet you." I'm still in so much shock, it comes out weakly, my voice slightly hoarse. Clearing my throat, I try to shake myself out of my stupor.

Wait! Did he say partner? Did the other guy say Dominic talked about me?

My heart is racing so fast. It feels like it's about to beat out of my chest. I'm fidgeting back and forth on my feet, not sure what to say. So many emotions are swirling inside my body. Dominic is here. He's back. I've tried to keep as little contact as I could with anyone from school, but I think I would remember if anyone mentioned he was coming to the reunion.

"Carla, are you okay?" His hand takes hold of mine, pulling me from the thoughts running rampant through my mind.

"Yeah, sorry. It's been a long day. What can I get for the two of you? Do you need a minute to look over the menu? Can I get you started with some drinks?" I ask nervously, holding the pen and pad in my hand, ready to write.

"Yeah, we'll each have a coffee and water." Dominic looks at me, his brows furrowed.

"I'll be right back." I turn and scurry away as fast as I can.

Holy fuck, he's here. What the hell am I going to do? What if Jake shows up? Thankfully, he has no clue that I put Dominic down as Brandon's father on the birth certificate. I just need to hold it together for the weekend.

Stepping into the back, I pull two mugs and two glasses off the shelf and set them on the counter. As I reach for the coffeepot, I accidentally hit one of the mugs and knock it off onto the floor, where it lands with a crash, shattering everywhere.

"That's coming out of your check, Carla!" Sal shouts from across the room.

"The hell it is! It's just a damn mug, Sal, not some expensive china," Martha hollers back at him as she steps up beside me.

"Are you okay? Did those two guys say something to you?" She pauses for a moment, watching me, as I set the coffeepot down and grip the counter, breathing deeply. "I'm going to kill someone. What did they do to you? Sal, get the bat!"

"No, no, no..." I rush out. Shit, she's got the wrong idea about what's going on. "That guy, the one sitting facing the bathroom, that's Dominic." There, I said it.

"The one who got away? Mr. Wonderful and daddy on the birth certificate?" All I can do is nod. My mouth has lost all ability to form words. She cackles in laughter as she fans herself. "This weekend has just gotten better. Oh yes, and girl, you didn't tell me how fine he was."

I just look at her, shaking my head. "He's gay. The hot guy sitting across from him?" I gesture in their direction. She turns and looks again, letting out a low whistle, still fanning herself. "That's his partner. So whatever ideas you're dreaming up in that head of yours, well, forget them."

"Did you ever think that maybe they swing both ways? You might still have a shot. The P between their D." She winks and giggles. Grabbing the remaining mug, she fills it with the coffee and heads back out to the counter, handing it to a truck driver sitting there. When she cocks her hip out, placing her hand on it, I know she is in full-blown flirt mode.

Taking a deep breath, I pull down two more mugs and restart the process of making their coffees, then pour their water. Once I'm done, I place everything on a tray along with a dish of various creamers, and make my way back out to their booth. Both of their eyes snap up to mine when I reach them.

"Here you go. Please be careful, as the coffee is very hot." I smile, trying not to look either of them in the eyes.

"If we burn ourselves, do you know someone who could play nursemaid?" the guy across from him asks; what was his name? Oh yeah, Chad. I catch Dominic moving out of the corner of my eye, just as Chad hollers ouch and starts laughing.

"Excuse me?" Is he insinuating having sex with me in front of Dominic? What an asshole.

"Nothing, Carla. Chad just has a very poor sense of humor. He thinks he's a comedian, but he's not. He should really stick to his day job. So, are you going to the reunion?" He looks at me with those same eyes from high school, the puppy dog ones, that just pull you in and make you want him. How I wish back then I would've let them.

"Yes, she is," Martha blurts out as she passes by the booth, acting like she is checking on a nearby table when she's really just being nosy.

"Yeah, I'm going, but I probably won't stay long." I sway back and forth on my feet as I reach up, slipping a stray piece of hair from my ponytail behind my ear.

"Oh yes, she is. She has a sitter for the entire weekend so she doesn't even have to come home,"

Martha blurts out yet again when she makes a random pass for no reason.

I'm going to fucking kill her! In the most vile, gruesome and painful of ways. She's going to suffer just like she's making me at this moment.

"You have a kid?" Dominic's piercing eyes look at me, as if he can see right through me and it's almost as if he's sad. Why would he be?

"Um, yeah, a boy, Brandon." *Why am I telling him this?*

"Yo, Carla, you got a phone call!" Sal shouts out from the doorway to the kitchen.

"I'll be right back," I mumble before turning. Only one place calls me here and it's the school.

Trying to be casual and not run from the table like I want to, I opt to walk briskly to the back. Picking up the phone, "Hello, this is Carla."

"Hi, Mrs. Sanderson, this is Mrs. Andric with Bellevelle Elementary. Mrs. Nelson wanted me to call you." An older, cracking voice comes through from the other end of the line.

"Is everything okay?" Worry fills me that there's been an accident and Brandon's hurt.

"Yes, she just wanted me to let you know that Brandon was complaining of a stomachache and had to make several trips to the bathroom this afternoon. She went ahead and sent him to the after-school program with Mrs. Davis but wanted you to know in case you wanted to pick him up early."

"Is he running a fever, throwing up?" Immediately, my mom brain starts jumping to everything that could be wrong, remembering there's a stomach bug going around. Not that I like my son being sick, but this may just be my reason not to go to the reunion this weekend.

"No, Mrs. Sanderson, he's not. Just complaining about his stomach."

"I'm on my way now. Give me about thirty minutes," I tell her before hanging up. Thankfully, we are not that busy and Denise is due in for her shift soon.

"Sal—" Turning, I see him already moving his hands, shooing me out.

"Tell Martha to get your tables until Denise gets here. I hope little man is okay." I love that I don't even have to explain. He knows if the school calls, it's important. For all this man's gruffness, he has a gentle and kind heart.

"I will." Heading to my small locker in our tiny break room in the back, I pull out my purse. Turning, I see Martha standing there, concern in her eyes.

"Is he okay?"

"Upset stomach. I'll know more when I get there. Can you get my tables? And no matchmaking." I add emphasis on that last part, giving her the mom voice that always works on my son.

She glares back at me like we're in a standoff at high noon. Neither one of us is willing to back down or be the first to give in. "Fine," she finally huffs out, crossing her arms across her chest. "But if they ask me anything, I may let these loose lips of mine tell them."

"In case you're wondering, the loose ones she's talking about are the ones on her face, not between her legs," Sal interjects. "Now let her get out of here and take care of Brandon."

I whisper a thank you to him, and rush out the back door, slipping around to the side of the building where I'm parked. I breathe a sigh of relief at not having to see Dominic again, thankful for the time to process him being here after almost eight years. He doesn't realize I saw him when he was in town, when his father passed away.

Please let me get through this week, I pray silently. Getting inside the car, I let out another prayer that it starts. After four attempts, it finally does, and I back out of the parking spot, heading to the school to collect my son.

October 2015

Pregnant! That's what those two little pink lines say. There's no way I'm going to get away from him now. As much as I know he doesn't want kids, once Jack finds out I'm pregnant with his baby, he'll never let me go. He controlled me from the moment I said yes to going on a date with him. Instead of going off to college and getting out of this town, I stayed here and went to the local community college with him. When he dropped out, or rather flunked out, I followed behind him at his command.

One semester, that's all the college experience I got. He immediately convinced me to move in with him, and that's when the abuse began. A shove here, a slap there. If I talked back to him, I'd get punched in the mouth. I got good at hiding it from my parents, not that they cared. Once I moved in with Jack, they packed and moved halfway across the country, and I'm lucky to even get a call on my birthday. It's like they forgot they had a daughter at all.

What the hell am I going to do? I'd been putting off taking the test for the last two weeks. But I knew I couldn't wait any longer, especially since my period was two months late. I've been walking down Main Street in a daze ever since I took the test in the drugstore bathroom. A plan is what I need, especially since Mary Ann Dupree walked into the drugstore just as the clerk was dropping it in the bag and her eyes zeroed right in on it. She's been after Jack for the last year and she knows just how much he doesn't want kids. Shit, she can have him.

Any time I've tried to leave him, I ended up in the emergency room. When they started asking questions, I would drive to the next town to get seen there. I was a klutz. It was Jack's answer for every injury I had, and there were a ton of them. But this baby can't go through that, so I have to save him or her.

Then it hits me. I'll tell him I cheated, that the baby isn't his. I can fudge a month. But what if he wants to know who I cheated on him with? Then it hits me. Someone who wouldn't be around to confirm or deny it.

Dominic was here last month when his father died. I went to the funeral, standing off towards the end of the cemetery behind a tree where no one could see me. He looked broken, and all I wanted to do was run to him and hold him, letting him sink into my arms as I console him. I didn't talk to him, but Jack doesn't have to know that.

No matter what it takes, I'm leaving Jack and saving this little being inside of me from a life of abuse, and if it has to be known, then Dominic Santini is his father. It's not like he'll be coming back here.

CHAPTER EIGHT

NIC

"Chad, really?" I make sure my face shows the irritation that I'm feeling toward him right now. "Did you have to be that forward?"

"Yes, I did," he replies matter-of-factly, and I just sigh in frustration. She rushed to the back to take the call, and the other server followed her. Carla still hasn't come back.

I open my mouth to speak, but he reaches across the table, takes my hand in his and squeezes it, comforting me. He taps me three times with his pointer finger, alerting me he's entering dominant mode and to behave. It's our own little alert we use when in public and not in the club scene.

"You'd never push the boundaries, Nic. So I took matters into my own hands. I'm going to continue to do it for the rest of the weekend. I don't want you going back home and regret not taking the chance. Do you understand me?"

I nod my head, but he clears his throat.

"I said, do you understand me, baby boy?"

"Yes, Daddy. But may I speak?" I keep my eyes lowered, like a good little boy.

"Of course. Now look at me while you talk."

Lifting my gaze, I look into his emerald eyes. Fuck, I love this man. His hair has grown out and is looking a little shaggy, and he's grown a beard, one I really hope he keeps. "I don't want to scare her away, and you heard her, she has a son. She's probably married."

We sit in silence, looking at each other, until we hear footsteps stopping at our booth.

"Hi there, guys. I'm Martha and I'm going to be stepping in for Carla. She had to step out." The sly wink she gives the two of us isn't unnoticed.

"Is everything okay? I heard her say she had a son?" Chad asks, and I already know what he's going to do.

"She does, and it will be. So I heard you went to school with her. Are you looking forward to seeing everyone you went to school with?" She aims the question at me.

"Not really, but I have no choice. My best friend bullied me into coming." I can't help the laugh that comes out.

"So I know you said Carla is going. Will her husband be with her? I know Nic was looking forward to spending more time with her, catching up." Chad thinks he's being sly, but he's not.

"She's not married, never was."

I'm seeing red. She had a baby, and the asshole didn't even think he should man up and marry her.

"Oh, okay, will her boyfriend or girlfriend be joining her?" I have to fight to keep from kicking him under the table again, with every question he asks.

"She doesn't have either of those," she answers with a laugh, then swats Chad with the pad of paper in her hand. "And for the record, she's into guys. Now, what can I get you two to eat?"

We give her our order, and she steps over to a table where an elderly couple has just sat down, speaking with them for a few minutes before heading back to the kitchen.

"Okay, she's single. So there's nothing to worry about. This weekend, you find out if there's anything between the two of you, and what that means for us as a trio." Chad's sporting a smile larger than his face, and I can't help but give him one back.

"But she has a son." I blow out a deep breath, rubbing a hand down my face.

"And?!"

I glare at him, my eyebrows drawn together. Doesn't he get it? She has a kid. We don't want to fuck her life up, and there's a father out there, one who may cause her trouble if she agreed to being with the two of us.

"Look, Nic, you know I love kids. Hell, you do too. We've even talked about adoption, surrogates, so her having a kid is perfect. And a son! What could be better? You know we'd make good fathers. I mean, aren't I already a good daddy to you?" This man is going to be the death of me. He's everything I could want and more. He wants to be a father, and he knows I do too. But I can't think about Carla right now. Getting my hopes up would gut not only me, but Chad as well.

Changing the subject, I ask Chad about his upcoming photo shoot for some magazine. He's pretty excited about it. He always is when it's something outside of our normal business. It makes him feel like he's really making it big, even though we're already successful. Millionaire's actually. But it's not something we advertise. We live modestly, with a few luxuries. Hell, why not enjoy a little? And each year, we allocate a huge portion of our profits to various charities. Our goal is to make the world a better place, better than the one I grew up in.

We're so lost in conversation we don't even notice the server has returned to the table with plates of food in her hands until she sets them down on the table. "Here you go. Two of our famous double-decker bacon cheeseburgers. I hope your cholesterol isn't high because this here will raise it." She lets out a deep belly laugh at her own joke.

"I'll be sure to get a check-up when we get home." Chad gives her a little wink and I swear to god she blushes.

"Young man, you look in perfect health to me. Now about this weekend. I want the two of you to make sure Carla enjoys herself. She's had some rough years, and she's gonna try to use the excuse of Brandon being sick to stay home. But I ain't gonna let that happen. Not on my watch."

"Brandon is her son? How old is he?" I ask.

"Yep, that's him, the perfect mix of angel and demon. He's seven, just had a birthday in April. He's a handsome little thing." She speaks about Carla and her son with such pride, but the mention of her having a hard life guts me. Even if nothing happens with us, I'm going to make sure she's taken care of; her and her son.

"We'll make sure she enjoys herself. In fact, we're going to the meet and greet at the school tomorrow night, then heading out to a bar afterward to hang with some friends. Maybe you can convince her to go with us. Actually, do you have a pen and piece of paper?" She rips a piece of paper from her pad and hands it with her pen to Chad. He quickly gets to work scrawling out a note, blocking it ever so slightly, so I can't see it, then hands it back. "Can you make sure she gets that?"

She opens the note and grins. "I sure can, honey. Now you two enjoy. Let me know if you need anything else." She winks and heads off to check on another table.

"What did you write?"

"I gave her your number, and might have said you had a crush on her in high school and haven't stopped talking about her. How you're looking forward to spending some time with her, then signed your name to it." He picks up his burger, taking a huge bite, still fucking smiling while he chews.

He's so proud of himself, I can't really be mad. Maybe it's a good thing. Either she reads it and calls or she ignores me all together. Either way, it brings me one step closer to having some type of closure.

Once we've had our fill, we head to the register, where Martha is helping another customer. When she finishes with him, we step forward to take care of our bill.

"How was everything?"

"Delicious. How much do we owe?" I pull my wallet from my back pocket, waiting for her to tell me the amount as I thumb through the bills I have in it.

"It'll be $25.69, hun."

I pull out a 20 and a ten, then have a thought. Thumbing through the other bills, I also pull out two $100 bills and hand it all to her. "Here you go Martha, for the amazing service and valuable information, as well as playing messenger with our note. Keep the change and split it with Carla. Just don't tell her it was from us."

She smiles brightly as she takes the money from my hand.

"Thank you, and I won't utter a word. I'll tell her it's credit card tips she somehow never got when Sal audited the records." She winks and sticks it into her pocket.

"Have a good day," we tell her, waving, as we turn and head back out to the car, ready to go check in at the Manor of Brighton Hill. Thankfully, it's also where the reunion is being held on Saturday night, so it will be super easy to slip away or not worry about having to drive to another hotel if I'm drunk.

As we drive through the town, I point out some of the sights to Chad. Brighton Public Library, my home away from home. We pass by Brighton High School and the school announcement board out front already has a message welcoming us. I show him where Boffman's is and tell him all about their world-famous ice cream. Before we know it, we're at the manor.

Chad pulls the car into a spot, and we both get out. He grabs our luggage out of the SUV and we head inside. I try to take the garment bag from him, but he just slaps my hand away. I love how this man takes care of me.

Stepping inside, we're hit with a refreshing blast of cool air as we make our way up to the counter. Standing behind is a woman that looks to be in her mid-fifties with brown hair and graying roots. She's wearing the loudest floral print top I've ever seen in my life, and definitely needs to be visited by the fashion police. Her attention is on the computer in front of her and whoever she is talking to on the phone. Glasses are perched on the tip of her nose, with a chain attached to each side that hangs around her neck. She looks up at us when we step up to the counter, holding up a finger letting us know she'll be right with us.

Finishing her call, she hangs up and smiles brightly at us.

"Hello! Welcome to Brighton Manor. How can I help you?"

"Yes, hi, I'm Nic Santini and I'm checking in. I have a reservation."

She looks down, flipping a page before looking back up at us. "Ahh, yes, here we are. I just need to see your credit card and then we can get you all checked in. It looks like you are here with us until Monday. Are you here for the reunion?" She takes my card and gets busy performing her check in routine.

"Yes, I am. Ten years just flew by."

"Wait a minute, Santini. Was your father Sylvester?"

"Yes, ma'am. He was."

"Oh, I'm Gladys. I took your reservation. He was such a sweet man. We all miss him around here. Here's your card back and your keys to your room.

You'll be in room fourteen. It's right upstairs and I'm including a map for you, just in case you get lost."

She hands me my card first and I slide it back in my wallet, then she places two keys in my palm. And when I say keys, I mean legit keys, not a key card. We have truly been transported back in time.

We head over to the stairwell, taking the steps slowly. As we are walking up them, I finally get Chad to relent and give me the garment and toiletry bag. It doesn't take long to make it to our room and Chad can't contain his laughter as I use the key to open the door.

"That is still the craziest thing I've ever seen. I hope we don't lose it," he says as we step inside of the room. It's spacious, with a king-size bed with a black-and-white checkered comforter on it. There's a dresser with a television and a vase of flowers, and as I get closer, I realize they are fresh, not fake. Guess Gladys really goes all out. There's an old rotary phone sitting on the nightstand by the bed, with five buttons along the bottom. The curtains are pulled, allowing the sunlight to shine into the room.

"How about a nap? Then we can check to see what Lorna and Kylo are doing tonight."

"Sounds good." Chad closes the blinds before stripping out of his clothes and pulling back the comforter. "Get undressed, baby boy, and come snuggle with me."

"Yes, Daddy." Following his orders, I swiftly undress and get in beside him, my body flush against his as I lay my head on his chest and my hand on his stomach.

We lie there quietly; him stroking my arm as I trace circles around his belly button. It's been a long day, and it doesn't take long for my eyes to become too heavy to hold open, pushing me into blissful darkness.

CHAPTER NINE

CARLA

"No, Martha!" No matter how forcefully I say it, she keeps shoving the money in my face. "It's charity and I'm not taking it. You served them. All I did was get them drinks before I left, so keep it."

"Girl, don't make me slap the stupid out of you. It's not charity and even if it was, ain't nothing wrong with accepting it. As for me, they tipped me too. So I have mine already. They seem like really nice men, so don't blow this chance at something."

"At what Martha? A quick roll in the hay, if they're even interested? This is my life, not some fairytale where the boy I should've given a chance in high school comes back and sweeps me off my feet like every sappy movie made in the eighties." I continue folding up the laundry from the dryer while Brandon sits in the corner reading a book.

His stomach problem wasn't because he was sick. No, apparently his friend, Andrew, had snuck a bag of Hershey Kisses from home and they ate the entire thing themselves. Ticked off was the very least of how I was feeling. Not to mention, I had to clean up the back seat of my car when he got sick on the ride home. Needless to say, he's banned from all snacks for the foreseeable future.

"Girl, you're the most stubborn person I have ever met. You're going to take the money or I'm going to stuff it down your throat. Now, shut your trap and listen. You have their number and I expect you to call it. They'll be at the meet and greet at the high school tomorrow, then they're going out for some fun, and you're going." She puts her hands on her hips as she stares me down, like a mother scolding her child.

Dropping the shirt I was folding back into the basket, I suck in a deep breath before blowing it out. I let my eyes roam over to Brandon, who's sitting quietly waiting for me to be done.

"Martha, he's only here for the weekend. I can't go there, not when I have him to think about." Gesturing my head in Brandon's direction. "Plus, I'm scared." There, I finally admitted it.

"Scared of what? Getting the best dick of your life, cleaning your pipes out? Or is it being with an actual good guy that has your panties in a bunch? It's time you live some of your life for you. It could be that you're the one he obsessed about and he's come to see if he has a chance, that maybe there could be something more." She looks at me with a cat ate the canary grin. She's not going to give up and I know it.

"Yeah, that's what it is." Fed up and not wanting to hear her anymore, I give in. "Fine, I'll go, but I'm not messaging him. If I run into him tomorrow night, then I'll go out to the bar with them. If I don't, then I'm coming home and going to sleep. But the money? I'm still not taking it."

She glares at me, neither of us batting an eye, not willing to be the first to back down. You could cut the air with a knife, it's so tense right now. I pick the shirt back up and go back to folding, keeping my gaze locked on to hers. Just when I think I'm going to win, she ups the game.

"Okay, you don't want the money, that's fine. I'll keep it." Then she turns to Brandon. "Hey buddy, guess what? Mommy got a big tip today and we're going to the movies, then pizza and ice cream, and finally, we're hitting the toy store." She turns her focus back to me, a huge shit-eating grin on her face. Martha 1 - Carla 0.

Brandon jumps up from the chair, his book toppling to the floor, hitting it with a thud, as he bounces around, fist pumping the air. He thinks he's escaping my no sweets mandate and he just may well be, but for the weekend only. I know no matter how much I put my foot down; the minute he steps in her door tomorrow, Brandon will get away with murder. Martha will let him do whatever he wants, especially since he has her wrapped around his little finger.

"You're terrible and also the very reason he's spoiled," I tell her curtly, as I continue folding my clothes. Inside, though, I'm laughing as I watch them dance around together, acting silly.

Fuck, how am I going to make it through this weekend?

Just seeing him today, after all these years, had my stomach fluttering with butterflies. You know the kind, when you're young and the guy is so handsome, sweet and then he gives you that smile that has your heart pounding.

The meet and greet. Maybe I can avoid him, and he'll never see me, then I can come right home. Then Saturday at the Manor. There'll be so many people, I can blend into the crowd. If I play my cards right, I can go the whole weekend without running into Dominic Santini, even if I would love to have him ramming his cock into me.

I shake off those thoughts before I get turned on right here in the laundry room. It's been so long since I've been with anyone, Brandon's father to be exact, that a cool breeze hitting me just the right way has my panties wet.

I fold up the last of the clothes and drop it into the basket. "Okay, buddy, all done. Ready to head upstairs? We still need to pack your bag for your weekend with Auntie Martha."

"Yes, ma'am." Jumping out of his chair, he runs over to me, just as Martha steps forward, reaching into her pocket. She pulls something out, gripping it in her palms out of my sight.

She sticks out her hand, taking mine in hers and slips the piece of paper into it, giving me a wink. I don't have to look. It's his number, I know it. My brain and my heart are at war at the moment, over wanting to call him. But for the moment, my brain wins out, and I slide it into my pocket. Picking up my basket, I head out of the laundry room and up the stairs, falling in behind Martha and Brandon, who are chatting away about their plans.

October 31st 2015

"Jack, can you come in here for a minute? I need to talk to you." I call out to him from the kitchen. He's sitting on the couch in the living room, beer in hand, playing a video game.

I know this isn't the best time to tell him, but I need to get it over with. I'm starting to show and I know I can't keep it from him much longer. He's made a few comments about the weight I'm putting on around my midsection. I'm three months along, but I've been stress eating like crazy, so it hasn't helped me with the weight.

"What the hell do you want?" he shouts back at me.

"I need to talk to you." I'm fidgeting my fingers like crazy. My nerves have my stomach all torn up inside.

"Then bring your fat ass in here. If I'd known you were going to turn into a fucking whale, I would've never moved in here. Hell, look at this place, it's a fucking pig stye. Didn't your mother teach you how to clean?"

I hold back the tears that are fighting to break free. The house is immaculate, other than his shoes strewn about the floor, and the littering of beer bottles on the coffee table. But of course, I'm the messy one.

Breathing in deeply, then blowing it out, I head into the living room. I've put this off long enough and I have a plan. I'm fully aware this night may not go the way I expect.

Sitting down on the chair, I brace myself for what's coming. "Jack, I need to tell you something, and it's not going to be easy."

He drops the controller on the coffee table, lifting his bottle to his mouth, taking a long swallow. "What?" he asks, his voice rough and cold.

"I'm pregnant." There, the best way to do it was to just rip the bandaid off.

"No, you're not. I told you I didn't want kids and you're on the pill and I wear a condom," he blurts out, his hands fisted.

Yeah, he wears a condom, unless he's drinking, which seems more often than not lately. As for the pills, well, I couldn't afford them any longer and had to stop getting them. I told him, and guess he forgot.

"I had to stop the pills when I couldn't afford my insurance any longer. I told you that. Don't you remember?" I barely get the words out of my mouth before he's in my face, slapping me.

"Bitch, you haven't told me shit. I would've remembered that. What did you do, punch holes in my condoms? You did this on purpose, because you wanted a kid. I bet it isn't even mine."

It's almost like he's given me the out I need, but before I can say anything else, he's grabbed a handful of my hair and jerked me out of the chair onto the floor. "That's it, isn't it? You've been out whoring yourself and now you want to pawn the bastard off as mine. You're getting a fucking abortion."

"No, I'm not." I spit out at him in anger. How fucking dare he even insinuate that.

"Yes, the fuck you are. I'm not raising someone else's kid."

"Then leave. But you're right, the baby isn't yours." Let him believe it. Please leave me, it's all I've ever wanted.

"Damn straight I'm leaving you, but not before you tell me who you opened your legs for."

"I'm not telling you anything."

He jerks me by the hair, just as his other fist lands in my face, knocking it sideways, as blood splays across the floor.

"Want to rethink that answer, cunt?"

"No," I force out through clenched teeth.

His fist lands on my face again, over and over until I black out. When I wake, he's gone, with every bit of cash we saved up. I manage to make it to the phone and call Martha, who comes and gets me, packing up all my stuff and taking me back to her apartment. It was the last time I saw him. The only good news I got was he left town after he managed to spread the rumor that I cheated on him and got pregnant, trying to pass the baby off as his.

That beating was the last he gave me, but it freed me. Never again will I let a man treat me like that.

CHAPTER TEN

CHAD

Waking up, my body is on fire. It takes a moment for my eyes to focus, but the once bright sunlight shining through the partially opened curtains is now replaced with a shimmering moonlight. Guess we were more exhausted than we thought. We slept right through dinner, and sometime into the night.

Looking down at my body, Nic's arm is draped over my abdomen as his head rests on my chest and his legs are thrown over me like I'm his own personal body pillow. No wonder I felt so hot. Lifting my arm that's resting on his back, I look at my watch, trying to see the time: two thirty in the morning.

Gently rolling him off of me, I sit up, letting my legs fall off the side of the bed as I run my toes through the carpeted floor. I rub the sleep from my eyes with the palms of my hand before standing up and heading to the bathroom to piss. I make sure to move quietly, not wanting to wake Nic. Being here is hard for him, especially with why he had to come home last time. He doesn't know it, but I've been handling things at his parent's gravesite. Nic thinks when we go, we're going to have a mess to clean up. I can't wait to see his face when he sees everything.

I want him to see this is a place he can return to when he needs to visit them. Not as a place that only holds bad memories of a bunch of stupid punk-ass high school kids. There are nights I stayed up long after he went to sleep imagining what kind of life we would have had if I'd gone to school with him.

Would he have come out earlier about being bisexual? Would I have received detention on a daily basis for coming to his defense until I was eventually expelled? Because there is no way I would've allowed those jerks to treat him the way he told me they did. In fact, I'm looking forward to meeting some of them tomorrow and seeing Lorna's little revenge plan fall into place.

Flushing the toilet, I wash my hands and step back into the bedroom. Nic is lying on his side, propped up on an elbow. His eyes trail up the length of my body with fire blazing in them. Fuck if he doesn't look delicious with the sheets draped over him, exposing that perfectly cut V that points directly to his cock.

"You left me." His husky voice whispers, like he's worried if he speaks louder, someone would hear.

Fuck if I care. I'm all for giving these vanilla people a taste of how good some delicious kink can be.

He rubs his hand across the bed in front of him, the very spot where I was laying before going to the bathroom.

"I was worried at first until I realized it was still warm." He bites on his bottom lip and my cock jerks in delight. Aching to be buried deep inside his ass, as he begs me to let him come.

"I'd never leave my baby boy. But seeing you there like that, I want to fuck you fast and hard. I want everyone in this place to hear you scream my name as I shoot my load deep inside your ass." Reaching down, I slide my boxers down my legs, my hard dick slapping back up against my stomach as I step out of them. Taking my cock in my hand, I grip it firmly, giving it a nice, slow stroke as I take Nic in.

"Whatever you want, Daddy." He lowers his gaze, so he doesn't look me directly in the eye. So obedient.

"Take off your briefs and then get on your knees. I want that ass waving in the air for me." My voice is deep and calm as I make my way over to him, enjoying how eagerly he follows my orders.

Taking my time enjoying the sight before me, I make my way over to our luggage to get some lube.

When I told him I wanted it quick and fast, I meant it. This weekend is for him, but I'm going to drag out his release, have him so worked up that when I get Carla to agree to be with us, he'll explode like he never has before.

Crawling on the bed behind him, I rear back and swat him across his ass. His muffled groan tells me he enjoys it, but he didn't listen. "Baby boy, I said I wanted everyone to hear you. Now how can they if you try to stifle yourself?" Once again, I smack his ass; this time he doesn't hold back, and god if it doesn't feel good.

Opening the lube, I squeeze some out along his crack, and rub my fingers through the liquid substance, spreading it down to his star, and around his rim.

I scoop up what's left and spread it along the length of my cock. Leaning over, I place a kiss on Nic's left ass cheek, a tender one, before I bite down hard. Mmm... this man is my everything.

Lining the head of my cock up with his hole, I push it inside, pausing long enough for him to relax before slamming deep inside him. His walls clench down on my cock and I have to breathe deeply to keep from shooting my load prematurely.

I stay still for a moment, allowing him time to accommodate my size, before pulling out, then thrusting back in, giving his ass cheek a firm slap as I do. His groans of pleasure echo through the room, just as the headboard hits the wall with the force I exert pushing into him.

"You like that, baby boy? How Daddy's cock feels inside this tight ass? The way I smack these rosy red globes of yours?"

"Yes, Daddy," he moans, his voice breathy.

I reach around his waist, taking hold of his hard cock; pre-cum already drips out of his slit, and I hum my approval. I love how excited and responsive he gets to my touch. Sad though, he won't be coming tonight. My hand moves slowly, stroking up and down his length, but he doesn't move, or attempt to buck his cock in my hand. My boy knows as soon as he does, this little attention I'm giving him is gone.

"Do you want to come, baby boy?" Releasing his cock, I place my hand across the small of his back and begin rocking my hips, thrusting in and out of him as he mumbles yes.

"What was that?" I growl, needing to hear him answer correctly.

"Yes, Daddy. Please let me come," he begs, and it only makes me harder. But my baby has something he has to do and until he does it, he won't be having a release.

"I love it when you call me Daddy!"

The sound of our skin slapping and the bed hitting the wall, as I fuck him like a jack rabbit fills the room. Hopefully, we're turning on whoever is in the room next to us, versus having to call around for a new place to stay tomorrow. Either way, with the way the walls of his ass are clenching around my dick, I'm going to be coming soon and it'll be worth it.

My balls tighten and I feel that familiar tingle. Grabbing his hips, I pump in and out of his hole faster, my thrusts becoming irregular until my cock twitches, shooting ropes of hot cum into his ass. My body locks up and my grip tightens on his hips, holding him in place as my cock jerks. Shuddering, I empty myself inside my boy.

I can hear his labored breaths, and I know he's dying for his own release. "You want to come, baby? You made Daddy feel so good."

"Yes, please. I need to come." The sound of his begging turns me on. If he isn't careful, he's going to have my dick primed and ready for round two.

Pulling out of him slowly, I roll him onto his back, still not giving him an answer. Standing from the bed, I walk to the bathroom, getting a wet washcloth and cleaning myself before returning to the room and doing the same for Nic. Tossing the rag on the floor, I crawl back into bed.

"Come here, baby." I hold the sheet up and Nic moves closer into my embrace, his hard cock pressed against my skin as I cover both of us up.

Rubbing his back, I pepper soft kisses on his head. His fingertip traces circles around my nipple, and even though he wants to ask for his release, he doesn't.

"I love you, baby boy, but you will not be coming tonight. Before you can have a release of your own, you need to deal with Carla. There's something there; I felt it at the diner."

"Chad—"

I pop his arm, shutting him up. "No, there's no Chad. If you want to come, then you'll find out this weekend if there's something there for you and Carla. For us. I love you more than words, but I want you to be happy. If including Carla in our lives will fill this void I know you have, then I'm all for it. You were right about her. Even in those few minutes, I could tell she's someone special, worth knowing. Now go to bed, baby boy. Tomorrow is a busy day."

"Yes, sir." He grips me tighter, and I close my eyes.

Friday June 2nd, 2023

"Thank you for making me come here. I don't think I would've done it on my own," Nic tells me as he replaces the fresh flowers with the ones in the vase on his parent's gravestone. "I wonder who put these here," he comments as he pulls them out of the vase, replacing them with the new flowers. "It looks like someone has been taking care of the plot."

"You're welcome, babe. You said your dad was loved, so maybe it's one of his friends doing it." Nic doesn't know I pay the local florist to deliver fresh ones every week, as well as ensuring the lawn is kept up. Since the plot was smaller, with only the loved ones of a few families buried here, I made sure to hire a lawn company to come and take care of it weekly.

"He was the best. I just wish I knew at the time he was working his fingers to the bone, mortgaging the house and taking out debt to cover what my scholarships didn't. Hell, he didn't even let me know. He led me to believe I had a full ride." Tears stream from his eyes now, finally letting some of the emotion he's kept bottled up inside about his father escape.

"Because he loved you. Your father was a smart man. He knew his son would be a success, and that's exactly what you are. He did what any parent would do, anything they could to help their child." I step in closer to him, wrapping my arm around his waist as he sinks into me, and we stand in silence for a few minutes.

Looking around, I'm happy to see it looking nice. I had no problem forking out the money to pay a company to come do it. A few rows of headstones, some with flowers, some without, but each one contains the history of someone special. People who need to be remembered, just like Nic's parents.

"I think we need to have some benches put in here, scattered around, so that people have somewhere to sit when they come to visit their loved ones. Then here, right in front of your parents, a special one dedicated to them. A place where we can sit with our kids and grandkids as you tell them stories about your parents."

He looks up at me, his eyes bloodshot and puffy from crying. "I think you're right. Let's make sure to take care of that on Monday. Being here with you feels right, and I want us to visit more. Not for this town or the people in it, but for them."

Kissing him on his forehead, I smile. I know a small piece of Nic's heart is healing at this moment.

CHAPTER ELEVEN

NIC

Senior Year October 10th, 2013

"Lookie what we have here," Jack croons out as he steps up behind me in the locker room.

I hate gym class. The worst part is that I'm stuck in here with the jocks, my biggest tormentors, and HIM. Jack Hendricks, the vilest of them all. He's a fucking tool. What Carla sees in him, I'll never understand. She could do so much better.

"Did you hear me, asswipe? I'm talking to you!" he shouts again through laughter.

Before I know what's happening, something strikes the back of my head, knocking it forward into the locker in front of me. The impact is so hard I see stars as I stumble back, crashing to the floor, the air knocked out of me.

I catch a glimpse of the football rolling around on the floor, no doubt the tool used in Jack's cheap shot. One of many he's taken on me over the course of my time here in this hellhole.

Before I can sit up, his shoe presses down on my chest. "Aww, did you fall down?" he taunts, laughing.

"Let me up, Jack." Trying to make my voice as deep and commanding as I can, as I squirm underneath the pressure of his shoe. But the more I resist, the harder he pushes down, until I can feel the air being cut off.

"I don't think I will. Not until I get a few things straight with you. You need to stop sniffing around my girl. Carla is mine and there's no way I'm letting some fucking nerd like you think you have a chance with her." Spittle flies, hitting my face with the last word.

"I'm not sniffing around her. We're fucking lab partners. That's it." I try to use what little energy I have to move out from underneath him, with no success.

"Oh, I know you're lab partners. It's the only time her ass is allowed to speak with you. But did you think I didn't notice you standing at her locker after third period? That goofy ass grin on your face as you looked at her with stars in your eyes. Do you really think she'd notice a skinny ass dork like you when she has me?" He grinds his heel deeper into my chest. "Stay the fuck away from her."

He lifts his foot from my chest and starts to walk away. Foolishly, I think I'm spared anything more. That is until he turns around and the impact of his foot collides with my side. I curl into a ball as he stands over me, laughing, taunting me about what will happen if I fuck up again.

Friday June 2nd Meet and Greet

God, I don't want to go to this shit. It's not that I'm scared of them. Hell, I'm a totally different person than I was back then. I've put on muscle, learned to fight, and I'm happy with who I am now. Confident in myself. I'm no longer the scared little boy they treated like scum.

Chad steps out of the bathroom, his hair still wet from the shower with a towel hanging low around his hips, exposing his trail of hair leading right to his cock. A moan escapes my mouth before I can stop it.

"Oh, baby boy. Later." He smirks, a lustful gleam in his eyes. "We don't have time right now." Heading over to our still unpacked suitcase, he pulls out a pair of jeans, much the same as what I'm wearing. While I chose to wear a white button up with a black blazer, he goes for a charcoal gray t-shirt and a black blazer. Both of us are sporting black boots. It was a low-key dress code for the meet and greet, but we didn't want to show up looking like total bums.

I can't take my eyes off of him as he dresses. The way his muscles flex with every movement has my cock twitching, and I swear I'm going to die if I don't come soon. Chad had some fun edging me earlier, closer and closer to an orgasm, only to stop just before I could shoot my load. But fuck if I don't love him.

"Lorna gonna be at the meet and greet or is she just going straight to the Eagles Nest?"

"She's going to the meet and greet. You know she has to make her grand entrance and ruin lives. I'm just going to sit back and watch the show and laugh. Those fuckers won't know what's coming, and it's gonna be hilarious." I can't help but chuckle as I zip up my leather snakeskin boots.

"Make sure to point the fuckers out to me, then maybe we can slip away and have some fun in the chemistry lab." He tucks his shirt in his jeans then zips them up, making his way over to me. Leaning down, he kisses me deeply.

"You can count on it. But they're nothing. It would be a waste of breath."

"I don't care. I still want to see the assholes who made my baby boy's life hell. Lorna may not be the only one getting some revenge this weekend." His face turns sharp as he clenches his jaw.

He's my protector and has been since that day in the library.

What the hell am I going to do? My meeting with financial aid didn't go like I expected. After this semester, I'm screwed. There's no way I can afford this place. How am I going to find a job to repay the remaining balance owed? I'm good until December, but come January, if I don't have some money, I'm out of here.

Dad had life insurance but with the additional mortgage he took out on the house, credit card debt, and bank loans, I didn't even break even. There was still money owed. I know he did it for me, and it makes me sick to my stomach, but I'm pissed off at him. If he had told me how much this school costed instead of lying and telling me I had a full ride, I would've gone somewhere else.

I needed to study, but the quiet of the library just afforded me more time to think, until finally I felt the tears coming. Picking up my books and bag, I rush to the back, slipping behind the last row of stacks that no one ever goes to, and slump down to the floor as I let all my emotions break free.

The tears fall down my cheeks, dropping to my shirt.

How can I be so ungrateful that I'm mad at my father for working his fingers to the bone to help me achieve my dreams? I'm so lost in my self-pity, I don't even notice someone squatting down in front of me until he speaks.

"Hey, are you okay?" His tone is soft and sultry. The sound hitting my heart like a rocket.

I want to speak, to tell someone everything, but all I can do is shake my head as I pull my knees to my chest and drop it down in my hands.

He sits down beside me and wraps his arm around my shoulders, turning me into him, and holding me. Being in his arms feels right; it's something I can't explain. It's like being with him is where I'm meant to be.

"Hey, whatever it is, we can figure it out. I'm Chad, by the way."

"Dominic," I manage to get out through sobs.

"Okay, Nic, here's what's going to happen. You and me, we're going to figure something out. First, though, I need you to dry those tears, then we'll get something to eat and go back to my place. Once you're calm, explain to me what's going on and we can make a plan. Are you good with that?"

Looking up into his piercing, emerald eyes, something clicks. Like no matter what, he can make it better, take care of me and I want to let him do it. He's so handsome, I have butterflies even in my moment of weakness. I've always been attracted to men, even acted on it once, but my heart wasn't with him. But this guy, this man, I suddenly feel a craving, a hunger for him. Realizing I haven't answered him, I nod.

"No, Nic. I need your words. Are you okay with what I offered?"

"Yes," comes out on in a whoosh of air as I let out a breath I didn't know I was holding.

"Good boy."

Why does hearing him say that make me feel good? Aroused. Shit, my dick is already twitching and all I need is for him to see a tent in my pants. Especially not knowing if he even likes guys. I have a gut feeling he does. But there's still that small sliver of a chance that he doesn't.

"Let me get my shoes, brush my hair and teeth and I'll be ready." Chad practically glides to the bathroom as he speaks, pulling me from one of the best yet worst memories of my life.

I nod, but quickly speak, knowing how much he hates when I don't use my words. "Okay. I'm going to shoot Lorna a text and let her know we'll be heading out soon. Wait until you get a load of what she's wearing. She's going to blow everyone's mind."

"Well, she is a stone-cold fox," he shouts back around his toothbrush, his voice muffled.

If I didn't know he thought of her like a sister, the same as I do, I might have felt a little twinge of jealousy. I love that Lorna has Kylo in her life; he is the yin to her yang, just like Chad is to me.

Me: We'll be heading over to the gym soon. When are you getting there? Your ass wanted me here, so you better not leave me hanging.

Lorna: We're already on our way. We should get there in about fifteen minutes. And you sir, are walking in attached to my arm. We're going to show those fuckers just what they're missing.

Me: God help me. I'll see you there. I'll be the hot guy with the even hotter porn star with him.

Lorna: I'll be the hot bitch, with all the tattoos, and the sex god with her.

Me: We are some lucky bitches then.

Lorna: That we are. See you soon.

"Hey babe, Lorna is going to meet us in the parking lot of the gym. Apparently, she wants to walk in together, arm in arm," I tell him as he steps back into the room.

"But I wanted to." He fakes a whiny voice and stomps his foot, like a toddler throwing a tantrum, making me laugh.

"Oh baby, you know you are always my arm candy and my daddy." Slipping my phone in my pocket, I stand up and make my way over to him, kissing him softly on his lips. He presses his firmly on mine, but I don't increase the intensity, instead I move over to his cheek, then ear, and last to that sweet spot on his neck that always gets him worked up. His very own little phone hotline to his dick.

"You better stop, baby boy, or I'm going to be ripping those pants off of you and taking that sweet ass of yours. We need to get going. You have a girl to see."

He winks before stepping away and smacking my ass, causing me to let out a yelp.

"Chad, I don't know. I know that Martha lady said she was single, and hinted to an attraction to me, but do we really want to pursue it?"

"Yes. Now stop procrastinating and get your ass over here." He picks up the room and SUV keys and opens the door, gesturing for me to exit the room. There's no use arguing when Daddy speaks. You listen unless you don't want to sit down for a week.

CHAPTER TWELVE

NIC

Standing in front of the school, I breathe in deeply and blow it out, trying to calm my nerves. I can't fucking believe I'm back at this hellhole, and I have the blue-haired beauty beside me to blame. She came to slay and damn if she doesn't look like she should be performing in some Latin ballroom competition.

"Ready?" She loops her arm with mine, giving me a smirk, knowing she's about to blow this reunion up.

"As ready as I'll ever be." Taking a deep breath, I step forward, with her at my side. Kylo and Chad, flanking us on either side. We look like one huge group, which will surely get the tongues wagging.

Stepping into the school, we head straight for the gym, ignoring all the looks we're getting. I imagine we are quite a sight and I have to wonder if any of them actually remember who we are.

"Did you give a picture of what you look like now?" I ask, wondering if she did, how it would work with her plan.

"Hell no. You?"

"Fuck no!" I bark out in laughter as we step up to the table in front, which has rows of nametags set on it. You can see gaps in between some of them, showing that there is already a significant amount of people here. I scan the names and see Carla still hasn't shown up. My heart drops a little at that.

"There you are, babe," Chad says as he picks it up and puts it on my jacket for all the assholes inside to see.

"There's yours, Lo." Kylo picks hers up and goes to put it on her.

"Nope. Absolutely not. I'm not letting anyone know who I am until the time is right. I got lives to blow up." She lets out an evil cackle before leading us inside the gym.

It's decked out in red and gold balloons and streamers, and there are tables lining the room with pictures on them. People are scattered around in groups and surprise, surprise, it would seem lots of the old cliques are already grouped back up. Guess time doesn't change much.

Strolling through the crowd, Lorna and our group smile and play nice, like we're all best friends even though we aren't.

"What time is Carla supposed to get here?" Lorna whispers softly in my ear.

"I don't know. Hell, I'm not even sure if she's coming. Chad left my number with the other waitress that was at the diner, but she hasn't called or texted.

My hope that she would be here plummeted when I saw her name tag still on the table."

We stop at the table with Abel and Rowan's picture on it. Of course, they would be put together. Their now picture is one of them together at one of their hockey games. Lorna and I both make a gagging sound at the same time.

"Are these two of the cunts who made your life hell?" Chad asks through gritted teeth, his hands fisted at his side.

"Yeah. But don't do anything, babe." I give him a look and he leans in, kissing me on the lips and my body goes limp; it's like my legs turn to jelly.

"I won't." He smiles innocently before glaring back at the pictures on the table.

Whispered female voices come from behind us.

"Did you see that? He kissed that guy and he's with a girl?"

"Are they all together? That's disgusting," one snotty voice says with repulsion. Lookin over my shoulder I steal a glance at who's speaking and see it's Nicole. She was a bitch. I guess that hasn't changed.

"Oh my god, Jan, is that Dominic? When did he turn into a smoke show?"

Lorna, finally having had enough while the rest of us just contain our hysterics, lets go of me and turns around, facing them. "Oh, you stupid bitch, he was always this hot. You were just too much of a skanky whore giving all the guys blow jobs under the bleachers to notice." She winks at me before sticking out her tongue and licking up the length of my face. "He's a fucking god in bed, too. Don't even get me started on how skilled he is at eating pussy."

Then, just to add a little fuel to the fire, Chad licks up the other side of my face. "And his cock sucking skills are unmeasured. He can make me come just by putting his mouth around it. In fact, I think I need it sucked now."

The trio of women gasp in shock.

"We'll meet back up with the two of you in just a little while." Chad takes my hand, pulling me away, and Lorna and Kylo laugh.

"Now, baby boy, where is this chemistry lab? I want to sit on the very chair you did, while you're on your knees in front of me, sucking my cock. You need to be quick because we still need to find Carla."

"Yes, Daddy, it's this way." I lead him out of the gym, straight toward the hallway that holds the science classes. Hope fills me that maybe, just maybe, he might be generous and let me come without seeing Carla yet.

Crashing sounds echo out through the hallway, getting louder the closer we get to the chemistry lab. Chad puts his finger up to his mouth, warning me to stay quiet, as we tiptoe to the door to peek through the glass panel.

Inside the room is a beautiful dark-haired woman, and she is demolishing the chemistry lab. It's like she's lost in her own little world, unaware of anything around her. "Do you know who that is?" Chad whispers.

I look again, really taking in her features this time before it hits me.

"Yeah, I think I do. It looks like Abigail. She was really smart and in a few of my classes. We never talked. Do you think we should go in and see if she's okay?"

He bites his lip as he raises his eyebrow, a tic I know to be his thinking face, before he responds. "No, baby boy, I think she's working through some shit. Maybe some crap that happened in her past. Now, you had biology with Carla too, right?"

"Yes."

"Good, let's give Abigail this room, and leave her to have her own little self therapy while we hit the biology lab, so you can suck my cock."

Taking his hand, I lead him down the hallway, away from the chaos Abigail was creating in the chemistry lab. Stepping up to the classroom door, I'm happy to see it's both dark and quiet.

Chad opens the door right in front of me and steps inside, flipping the lights on. Walking in behind him, I look around. The chalkboard still holds the last message of the year the teacher wrote, telling them to have a good summer.

Once I'm further inside the room, I'm assaulted with the smell of cherry blossom. The same scent that was always on Carla. It makes me stop for a moment to glance around, thinking she's here. But she isn't. It's merely the memory hitting me.

Chad's taking his time strolling around, letting his fingertips dance along the tops of the tables. "You know, I was always good at biology," he says. "I loved learning about the human body, especially the male one."

"I'd say you learned it exceptionally well. Especially how to arouse it. Bring it to the highest of highs and then crumble under your feet."

"That I do, don't I, baby boy? Now tell me, which one of these was your seat." He waves his hand around the room, glancing back at me with his eyebrow raised.

I take my time, drawing out the anticipation of what's about to happen. Weaving in and out of the tables, until finally stopping at the one I sat in. "Here."

Chad makes his way over to me, placing his hand on the one beside me. "And Carla sat here."

I nod.

"I've changed my mind. I'm going to sit in Carla's seat while you suck my cock. But I want you to think about her while you're doing it. Of eating out her pretty pussy as her juices cover your mouth. The image of your tongue licking through her wet folds, nibbling on her delicious little clit. Can you do that, baby?" He undoes his pants, freeing his hardened dick, pre-cum already beading at the slit. "Make sure nothing gets on my pants. Understand?"

"Yes, sir."

"Good, now on your knees and suck me, baby boy."

I drop quickly, not even caring about the pain radiating through my knees as they hit the floor. I take his cock in my hand, rubbing my thumb over his mushroom head, smearing the pre-cum along his shaft, and slowly start pumping up and down.

"That feels good, baby, and I love it, but your mouth isn't on it." His voice is stern as he reaches out and takes hold of my head, pulling my mouth to his cock. Opening wide, I slide my mouth down his shaft, stopping along the way to relax my throat, so I can take in more.

"That's it, baby boy. Suck Daddy's cock. Make me come. You're such a dirty boy, sucking me off where anyone could walk in and see." His hand still on my head grips my hair, forcing me up and down, and he groans.

"Fuck yeah, baby boy. When we get our girl, you're going to have to teach her just how Daddy likes it."

I can feel my dick straining against the zipper of my pants, begging to have my hand wrapped around it, pumping up and down. But like a good little boy, I don't do what I desire. The reward of being obedient far outweighs the pleasure of coming at this moment.

"You're doing so good, baby boy, but you need to make Daddy come. We've got to go find our girl and get back to Lorna. We don't want to miss the show once Lorna reveals herself. Now make Daddy come." His words become forceful at the end.

Moving my head with the help of his hand, I bob up and down his shaft. Taking his length deeper and deeper, my moans vibrating off of him.

"Ah fuck, baby boy, I'm going to come. I want you to swallow down every drop. Don't let any escape."

And I don't. I suck him dry, enjoying every bit he has to give me. Only when he's empty do I release him, helping him put his cock back in his pants.

"Okay, let's get back." Chad reaches out and takes my hand in his, helping me up.

Leaving the classroom, I stop at the door, taking one last look back, happy with the new memory I added to this room. Chad is helping slowly to chip away at all the bad ones. As we walk down the hall, the sounds in the chemistry room have been replaced with moaning. Guess she found someone to help her alleviate whatever was built up in her in another way.

"Why are you smiling?" Chad asks, squeezing my hand.

"I'm just happy to be here with you," I tell him.

"Me too, baby boy."

We make our way back to the gym, sidling up beside Lorna and Kylo, who are talking about how they're ready to get the hell up out of here. Following her gaze, I see Abel and Rowan, where they stand holding court across the room with some of their old minions from high school.

CHAPTER THIRTEEN

CARLA

"Thanks, Chip, you're a lifesaver," I tell him as he pulls to a stop in front of the high school. My car picked tonight to not start, and I was thanking the Lord for answering my prayers. I didn't have to come tonight. But nope, Martha was having none of that and called Chip to pick me up. Even paid the fare, leaving no reason for me to not attend tonight.

"Happy to be. Plus, you just made me one step closer to that new ride of mine. Have fun and if you need me, you have my number. Make sure to call early; I have a feeling I'm going to be a busy man this weekend." I slide him a tip as I exit the rear passenger door of his blue wood panel passenger van. My eyes linger on the joker smile tattoo on his right hand. He was always my favorite character, even though he was the bad guy.

Once I'm out of the van, I give him an awkward wave as he pulls off, no doubt headed off to pick up his next ride. Taking a deep breath, I know it's now or never. Either I walk through those doors right now or I'm going to become a chicken shit and run, hiding out somewhere, before eventually making my way home. Of course, I'd have to come up with some bogus story about what happened tonight to satisfy Martha.

Pulling on my big girl panties, I open the doors and step inside. There are a few people scattered about, but I keep walking forward until I come to the table with all our names on it. As I search through the names, I pick up my tag and put it on, but I keep looking. I need to know if he's here. I pass over name by name. Jack's is still laying there, thankfully, but Dominic's is gone. Which means he is already here.

Breathing in deeply and slowly blowing it out, I open the gym door and step inside. I scan the crowd, looking for the one man I came here to see. I'm filled with both worry and relief when I don't spot him, but then out of the corner of my eye, I see him. He's standing arm in arm with a woman with blue hair. There are two men on either side of them, one of which is the man from the diner yesterday. Dominic has his head thrown back, laughing at something one of them said, and I know at this moment I've misread the situation. Maybe they weren't together, he's with her. Or are they all together?

I keep to the outskirts of the room, taking my time, stopping at each of the tables to look at my classmates' then and now pictures. Many haven't changed at all, but a few have, like Dominic.

Instead of the once shy, meek boy now stands a strong, confident man, and I'm happy for him. Me, well, I went from the girl who used to hang with the popular crowd, thanks to my boyfriend, to the outcast that people whisper about, thanks to him again.

Stopping at the table with Dominic's picture, the first thing I notice is he doesn't have a current one. I wonder why? Why no one saw the amazing person he was in high school, I'll never know. He was kind, sweet, handsome, and when you could get him to open up to you, funny. It was always known he would be successful and by the way he's dressed, I'd say he lived up to it.

"He's still as handsome, isn't he?" a soft feminine voice says from behind me. I look over my shoulder to see the blue-haired beauty.

"Oh, yeah. We were friends in high school," I whisper nervously as small beads of sweat break out on my forehead.

"I know." Her words send me for a loop.

"He told you?" Why would he tell her? For that matter, why would he want to see me here if he's with someone, two someones if what I saw at the diner is true?

"No, I'm his best friend, Carla. Don't you recognize me?" She smiles at me, laughing softly.

I look closer at her now. Taking in all of her features, trying to recall her name. Then it hits me.

"Lorna," softly escapes my lips.

She nods her head while placing her finger to her lips, shushing me.

"I don't want all the puppies and kitties to know who I am yet. But how about we get you over to Nic and Chad? They'll be so happy to see you."

She links her arm with mine, moving through the crowd like she owns the room, heading straight for the three men across the room.

Snickers and whispers about me filter into my ears.

"Can you believe she's here?"

"She should be fucking ashamed of what she did to Jack."

"He's better off without her skank ass."

"Don't pay any attention to them. They're just jealous cunts that don't have a life. Karma's a bitch, and they'll get what's coming to them," Lorna whispers into my ear, while giving everyone we pass a look that could kill.

We keep going, and the closer we get, the stronger the butterflies fluttering in my stomach get.

"Look who I found!" she calls out as three sets of eyes snap over to me.

"Hi." I wave awkwardly. Come on, Carla, could you be any more of a geek?

"You made it. I was afraid you weren't coming, especially since you never messaged." Nic moves closer to me before wrapping his arms around me in an awkward hug. Guess I'm not the only one nervous.

My hands instinctively wrap around his waist, tucking my head into his chest.

"What a slut!" a blonde says loudly as she walks by.

"Who, you? Yeah, I know you are. I just wasn't going to say anything. I can hear your pussy lips flapping right now. You might want to go check on vaginal rejuvenation. Sex with you surely isn't any fun for your partner," Chad blurts loudly, defending me, causing us all to laugh.

I pull away, regaining my composure. Lorna taps Nic on the shoulder before gesturing her head in the direction of—wait, is that Abel and Rowan?

Chad raises his voice, making it deeper as he speaks, ensuring anyone near us can hear. "Ready to go to the Eagle's Nest, Dominic? Lorna said she was going to drink us under the table." Looking over, I see both of them, listening in rapt attention.

"I sure am. Are you coming with us, Carla?" Nic asks, and I just look at him. Nervous and unsure of what to say.

A hand comes around my shoulder, as Chad's playful, honey voice rings in my ear. "Of course she is. Did you want to ride with us? We can bring you back to your car."

"Oh, I didn't drive. I got a ride here. My car wouldn't start." Why am I telling them all of this?

"Perfect, then it's settled. You'll ride with Nic and me, and we'll make sure you get home safe." He keeps his arm over my shoulder as Nic takes my hand, leading us outside. It's only then I notice Jack standing with Abel and Rowan. His eyes focused on me as he glares with pure hatred.

"Shots, shots, shots!" Lorna chants behind us as we exit the gym.

I can't believe I'm doing this. I'm actually getting into a car with a boy, hell, a man now, that I've thought about for years.

"Hand me your name tag, Carla. I'll put it with mine in the car. I'm tired of wearing it already," Dominic, I mean Nic, says. Shit, I really need to get the name right.

Nic, Nic, Nic. I repeat it over and over in my head and damn if it doesn't have a nice ring to it.

"Would you like to ride in the front or the back?" Nic asks.

"Huh?" I mumble, caught off guard. I know he asked me a question, but my brain doesn't want to process an answer. "Oh, the back. I can sit in the back."

"Okay then." He opens the door as Chad finally removes his arm and heads around to the driver's side.

"We'll see you there," Chad shouts out to Lorna and the man she's with. Hell, I hadn't even got his name yet.

Sliding into the back seat, Nic gives me a wink before he shuts the door and gets in the front passenger seat as Chad slides into the driver's seat.

"So I know Martha said she's watching your son this weekend, but do you have a time you need to be home by?" Nic turns around in his seat as Chad starts up the SUV.

"No. But you don't need to worry about getting me home. I can call Chip to come get me."

"Chip? Is that your boyfriend? I thought you were single?" The questions fly so fast from both of them, I don't really know who asked what.

"No. I am. And he's just a local cabbie." I laugh. When they both sigh, I have to squeeze my legs together to ease the throbbing in my core. Why does that turn me on?

I sit silently as we ride to the Eagle's Nest. My eyes catch Chad reaching across, grabbing Nic's, and I feel like the third wheel. I can feel the sexual tension between them. The way he lifts their joined hands up to his mouth and looks at him has a soft gasp escaping before I can stop it. I know they heard. But thankfully they don't let on like they did.

My core is pulsing. The vision of being caught between the two of them in the throes of passion nearly has me moaning without anything being done to me. I haven't been with a man since Jack. Would it be bad to take one night and enjoy it if they were to offer, like Martha seems to think?

Would I be able to keep my emotions out of it and not fall for them? Hell, Dominic already consumes a huge portion of my thoughts.

"You're quiet back there, baby girl. What's on your mind?" Chad asks.

"No-no-nothing," I stutter, rubbing my thighs together, trying to ease the intense throbbing between them.

"Don't lie. The way you're squirming, I'd say you're all worked up and need some relief. Do you want Nic and I to help you?" They both turn and look at me with heat in their eyes.

Do I want them to? One night. That's it. No strings. Just some good old-fashioned sex. "Yes," I spit out before I change my mind.

"Then promise to stay the night with us. We'll have some fun at the bar, then head back to the Manor and have some fun in bed."

All I can do is nod my head.

"Words, baby girl. I need words. Before we do anything tonight, Nic and I need to sit and talk with you."

"Okay." I know the one word answers aren't giving them much, but right now, it's all I have.

CHAPTER FOURTEEN

CHAD

She responded so well to being called baby girl, not even flinching. I'm hopeful once we talk and tell her about us, she'll accept us. Then after tonight, I'll have my baby boy and girl and we can convince her to come live with us.

The way she fidgets in her seat, her skirt riding up higher and higher revealing more of her thick, luscious thighs as she moves has my cock stirring in my pants. Glancing into Nic's lap, I see his is, too. Fuck, I would love to have him in my mouth right now, or see my baby girl taking his cock into her mouth, bobbing up and down on it with her ass up in the air.

Fuck me! My mind is already making plans for tonight. Because my girl will accept us and be a part of what we have together.

I'm so lost in my plans, I don't even realize the GPS is directing me to turn into the parking lot of the Eagle's Nest until Nic is telling me I'm about to miss my turn. Somehow, Lorna and Kylo beat us here. He has her pinned against the building as they make out like two teenage kids. Pulling into the open parking spot in front of them, I decide to hang out the window and give them a little catcall.

Lorna, being who she is, just laughs as Kylo releases her, then takes a bow and turns so she can flash her barely covered ass.

"That's your best friend," I say, shaking my head at Nic.

"I know, and I love every bit of her crazy ass." He sticks his head out the window and hollers at her. "That's my bitch!"

Turning off the SUV, we all get out. A smile crosses my face when I see Nic take Carla's hand in his. I can tell she's nervous. It's obvious. Her quickened breath, the way she sways back and forth, and the sheen of sweat on her forehead. My heart races, knowing we're going to have her sweating for a whole different reason tonight.

"Okay, I need a drink and to dance." Heading over beside Nic, I take his hand and we all go in together, following Lorna and Kylo.

Headlights flash on us as I step in the door, and I have no doubt that another part of Lorna's plan is about to be put in place. I know the fuckers overheard me. That was the whole point, anyway. She wanted them here. To embarrass them in front of people and swoop in as the savior.

Nic whispers something to Carla and she lets out the cutest little snort and fuck I never believed in love at first sight, other than with Nic. But if it's real, then it's struck me twice, because this woman has already weaseled her way into my heart.

Stepping inside this place, it's definitely a dive bar, the best kind of bar there is. There are tables scattered about, with a couple of pool tables, darts, and a dance floor smack dab in the middle with a DJ stand up on a small makeshift stage.

We all head straight for the bar and order a round of tequila shots. Lorna, of course, pays compliments to the Dynamic Duo of idiots. Speaking of, just as I turn around, they stroll inside with that loser Jack and I'm itching to drag his ass out to the alley and beat his ass senseless. I find the thought of him pinned underneath me, begging and crying for me to stop funny.

"What are you laughing at, babe?" Nic asks.

"Payback." One word, but it says a million things.

Both Nic and Carla's eyes follow mine and land on what has my attention. It doesn't escape me, the fear that's present in her's. Which one of those three put it there?

"Let's dance," Nic tells her as a slow song comes on. He pulls her out to the dance floor, Kylo and Lorna following suit, as I lean back against the bar and watch. My cock grows hard as Nic grinds his body slowly against hers.

I feel the air shift beside me as someone takes the seat next to me. Someone who is wearing an ungodly amount of cologne. A knock off brand at that. Turning back to the bartender, ignoring my guests, I order another round of shots. This time, I'm sure to pull out my black American Express card, being sure to flash it to the three men seated beside me.

The beat of the song changes and Nic and the rest of them make their way back over.

The trio next to me orders a round of drinks and I'm laughing inside. We all take our shots as Lorna orders another round. Man, I need to slow down or we may still be calling Chuck—no, that's not it—Chip. Yeah, we'll be calling Chip to take us back to the manor.

Lorna keeps eyeing the men beside us, and I know we are about to get a show. Sure enough, the bartender heads back our way, placing our shots down in front of us with a smile before turning to them with a scowl.

"Do you have another card? This one was denied." Her voice is blunt, while they have looks of confusion.

"You must be wrong. Run it again." I remember from the picture and from seeing him play hockey, that it's Abel speaking.

"I did, sir, and it was still denied. So, as I said before, do you have another card?" she juts her hip out as she tosses the credit card on the counter.

"I got it, man." Rowan pulls out his wallet, taking out a card and hands it to the bartender. "It must just be a glitch with you being out of town."

"Yeah, that's it. You better believe I'm having a word with them first thing in the morning." He scoffs, as Lorna snickers so softly no one can hear.

"Could we get another round of shots when you come back?" I call out to the bartender, who just nods her head and gives me a thumbs up.

We go about our conversation, all while eavesdropping on the trio beside us as Abel bitches about his card. I try not to look, but I can see how Carla is cowering beside Nic, almost like she's trying to hide. Catching a glimpse out of the corner of my eye, I see Jack still glaring at us, jaw clenched and pure anger on his face. He has a blonde with him, very pregnant, I might add, who looks exhausted. It's only then I notice the ring on his finger, one that matches hers. She must be his wife.

The bartender comes back, sets the tray with our shots on the counter and passes them out, before stepping over to the guys and hands back Rowan's card. "This one was also declined. How are you planning to pay for the drinks you already drank?"

Lorna takes that moment to act. Sliding off of her stool, she walks behind us, slipping in between the two of them.

Once she's done, she comes back, downs her shot, and takes Kylo's hands. "Let's dance biotches!"

We all get up and follow suit. Nic and I make a Carla sandwich as we grind on her to the dance music.

The heat between us is unmatched. I know she is the final piece to our puzzle, the one that completes us and makes us whole. If she accepts us, there is no way in hell we're leaving here without her and her son.

I can feel my back burning and I know we're being watched. And if I had to guess, the eyes on us would be Jack.

Leaning in closer, so that both Nic and Carla can hear, I whisper loud enough for them to hear. "Are you two ready to get out of here?"

They both nod, and I turn back to Lorna and Kylo. "Lorna! We'll see you two tomorrow. Try to stay out of trouble." I wink at them before taking both Nic and Carla by the hand and weaving through the crowd.

We pass by the trio, and I notice the pregnant blonde is missing.

"What a slut. Look at her, opening her legs for two of them now. See, this is why I cut her loose, especially when she tried to pawn that kid off as mine," Jack spits out to anyone who can hear, and I just so happened to be one of them.

Letting go of Carla's hand, I place it in Nic's. "Get her outside to the SUV, babe. I'll be right there."

"Chad, don't. He's not worth it," Nic pleads with me, but I've had enough of this shit and I plan to make it known.

"Do as I say." My words are more forceful this time. He shrugs his shoulders, but when the dominant in me comes out, he obeys.

I see Kylo watching out of the corner of my eye, and I know he'll have my back in an instant. But I don't plan to get bloody before Nic and I have a chance to talk to Carla.

Stepping up to them, I give him a once over, typical punk ass kid who turned into a jerk off adult. "Did you say something disparaging about the lady with me and my partner, my husband?"

He just looks at me, stupefied, not saying a word.

"Oh, I'm sorry. Did you not understand the question? Let me dumb it down a little bit for you. Were you talking shit about the lady with me and my husband?"

He steps up, finally getting a backbone, and I can only assume he thinks the two hockey players with him are going to have his back. But from the looks on their faces, as Kylo and Lorna step closer, I'd say that it's a no. They've already had enough embarrassment tonight.

"You mean the slut with you that used to be my ex-girlfriend? The one who cheated on me and then tried to pass the kid off as mine. Then yeah, I am. If I was you, I'd run as fast as I could."

"Looks to me like she won. She's free of your loser ass and has us now."

"She's just looking for a paycheck. I'd make sure you wear a condom for more than just preventing catching a disease. She'll try to get knocked up, especially after seeing that card of yours. All that whore sees is dollar signs." He laughs, thinking he made a joke, and I so happily give him a false sense of security when I join in.

But only briefly. My hand flies out, taking hold of his and twisting it behind his back before dropping him to the ground. I let go long enough to give him a firm punch in the kidney.

"How naïve are you, Jack? You see, Nic and I are the winners here, especially if she ends up pregnant. Now say another fucking word about her and you'll be leaving this bar on a gurney." I spit on him before turning and walking away, spotting his wife exiting from the bathroom.

"If I were you, I'd divorce his ass. You could do better." She just looks at me before turning her head.

Seeing him on the floor, she rushes over to him as fast as her legs will move. Lorna and Kylo throw me a thumbs up, while Abel and Rowan just look on, unsure what to do.

Maybe those two have a little common sense after all.

Now it's time to take my man and woman home. We need to have a little chat before we have fun.

CHAPTER FIFTEEN

CHAD

The ride to the manor is quiet. Nic's anxious about confessing to Carla how he felt and still feels. And me, well I'm nervous about if she'll accept us and our lifestyle. But as I park the car, I know it all comes down to what happens in the next thirty minutes.

"Let's head to the room. We have some stuff to talk about." It's why I didn't want to stay any longer. Lo would have gotten us drunk and my baby girl needs a clear head when we tell her what we want. About our lifestyle.

Hand in hand we stroll inside the manor, and I notice the sly grin Gladys, the innkeeper, gives me. *Wait. Is she giving me a thumbs up?* That sly lady, I may just need to slip her a card for a one time free pass to one of our clubs. I have a feeling it's right up her alley.

Stepping up to the door to our room, I reach in my pocket and pull out the old school key. I'm still in disbelief that they use these here. But hey, it beats the key cards that always seem to deactivate in one way or another.

Carla's nervous as she steps inside the room, with Nic following her. I'm the last to walk inside, shutting and locking the door behind me. I can't believe she's actually here with us. The thought that we could have her is becoming more of a reality. Nic guides her over to the bed and helps her sit on the edge, with him taking the spot beside her. Pulling over a chair, I put it right in front of them and take a seat.

"We need to talk first, Carla. There are things you need to know so you can make an informed decision. Nic, baby, you need to start."

Nic takes a deep breath before turning his body, pulling one of his legs up on the bed so he can face her. "Shit, this is hard," he says, blowing out a big breath as he reaches out, taking her hand in his.

"I can leave," comes softly from her, causing a small pang of pain in my chest.

"No, it's not that. I very much want you here. Fuck, this isn't coming out right. I've loved you from the moment you sat beside me in science class that first day. I always thought it was just a high school crush, but it never went away. I even told Chad all about you. Even now, I feel the same as I did then."

She looks at him, her eyebrows raised in confusion. "But aren't you and Chad together? Married?"

"Yes, we are. Happily, in fact, but we've always had something missing in our relationship. It's you," I tell her, putting Nic out of his misery.

"You want me to be with the both of you?" She moves her finger between the two of us with wide eyes.

"Yes. In every way imaginable. We want you as our third, living with us, mother to our children." I could go on and on, but I know what I've said probably already has her mind racing.

"But my son—" Before she can finish, I stop her.

"Will be ours. Honey, you are a package deal, one that we want. There's no way we would take one without the other. We actually want to meet him, but that is something we can discuss tomorrow. We have more to tell you."

"Carla, do you know what I do? How I make my money?" Nic asks, and she shakes her head. I'll let it go for now, but baby girl needs to learn to use her words.

"Do you want me to tell her, Nic?" I offer, trying to make this easy for him if I can.

"No, I can." He takes a deep breath and rubs his thumb along her hand as he holds it.

"What is it? It can't be that bad. You're not like some hired assassin, like in a romance novel, are you?" She lets out a little laugh as she asks, and I can see Nic smile. She's done a small part to calm his anxiety.

"So what I do goes back about eight years. I'd just lost my dad and found out how far in debt he went to help ensure I could go to the college I wanted. All along, I thought I had a scholarship that gave me a full ride, but I didn't. I was distraught and didn't know how I was going to pay for the remainder of my summer tuition. Then I met Chad." He pauses and looks at me, so I pick up where he left off.

"He was so upset, so lost, and my heart called out to him, a need to take care of him. I brought him back to my dorm room, and explained to him what I did for money. My family wasn't wealthy. Hell, I was the first person to go to college. When fast food jobs weren't cutting it, I started modeling, which led me down a road to starring in porn. I was tested monthly and wore condoms. It didn't hurt that I worked for a reputable company. I don't want you to worry that if things progress with us, you could catch something.

We will gladly show you our clean bill of health or be tested for you ASAP."

"You do porn?" she asks, her eyes wide in shock, and I'm almost afraid we're going to lose her.

"I did. We did. We were even in demand and paid well. It allowed us to save money. My major was business and Chad's was photography. Investments came easy to me and over the period of two years, I made us very wealthy. So much so that we bought the company we worked for, then began building a string of clubs, ones geared to our lifestyle." Nic shifts again where he sits, licking his lips that have become dry.

"What are you trying to tell me? You own a porn company? You do porn? What kind of club? Are they porn clubs?" she spews out a series of questions, one after the other.

"No, not porn clubs. Chad and I live a particular lifestyle. One of the dominant-submissive." Nic clears his throat. "There are many kinds. There are caretakers, traditional, pet, hell, I can go on and on. But for us, well, it's about me giving up control to

Chad and knowing he will take care of me. We have things we like sexually, which we want to share with you. But you never have to do what you don't want. We have a stop light system. Green is good, yellow you're okay but be cautious, and red, well that's stop."

"Okay." That's it? We bare our souls to her and she says okay.

"Carla, you should also know that while we don't star in porn regularly, every once in a while we still do, but if you are with us, there's no need for us to. It was merely a way for us to fill a small hole that was still there, one that was waiting for you," I tell her.

"How does this work? All of us together," she asks as I scoot forward in the chair, reaching out and pushing a stray strand of hair behind her ear.

"You let us please you. Bring you to such orgasmic highs, just as you will us. But first, I'd like you to give up a little control to me. Let me be your daddy and you be my baby girl. Be good and I'll let you come. Can you do that?"

She nods her head, and I growl.

"First thing you learn, sweetie, is to always use your words. You didn't know, so there will be no punishment, but in the future there will be. Do you understand?" I ask her again, more sternly.

"Yes."

"Yes, what?"

She looks confused for a minute, casting her gaze to Nic, then back to me. He gives her hand a reassuring squeeze, filling her with some confidence she may have been missing.

"Yes, Daddy."

My cock goes hard.

"That's my baby girl. So good. What color are we?"

I can see her think for a minute before she replies. "Green, Daddy."

Fuck me.

"I want you to stand and take off your clothes. Let me see my girl. Nic, baby, you do the same."

"Yes, Daddy," they answer in unison.

Nic stands and begins to remove his clothes slowly. Carla is a little more hesitant, but obeys just the same.

She's beautiful. She's removed her dress, standing before me in a black bra and panties that have seen far better years. A shopping trip is in order for my girl. She's going to be lavished like the queen that she is.

"You're gorgeous, Carla. Isn't she, Nic?"

"Yes, Daddy. None can compare to her. Never have."

Nic is now naked, but Carla still hasn't removed the final articles of clothing.

"What color are you?" I ask, needing to know before I proceed any further.

"Green," she pauses, then smiles. "Daddy."

"Good girl. Nic, help her out of her underwear, then lay her on the bed." He jumps into action, just like the obedient boy he is. Reaching down, I undo my pants and pull out my hard cock, gripping the shaft with the palm of my hand, slowly pumping up and down at the sight before me. Not too fast, nice and slow; I want this to last.

"Bend her legs up, baby, and spread them. I want to see her pussy."

He lies down beside her, his cock rock hard, but not once has he tried to touch. Something I fully intend to reward him for later.

He pulls her legs apart; her glistening pussy is on display.

"Take your tongue and tease her, suck on her nipple for me, while you slide your fingers through her wet folds."

Carla arches her back up at the first touch of Nic's mouth on her, and her gasp turns into a moan. One that she's been aching for. She's going to come fast, but that's okay. It's about her becoming comfortable with us, and Nic exploring her. He should have her first. She was his first love. My mind is already thinking about tomorrow night and what I have planned for my baby boy and girl.

"Baby girl. Can Nic fuck that sweet pussy of yours?"

"Yes, Daddy," she cries as he pulls on her nipple with his teeth. At the same time, he taps her clit, then pinches it hard.

"Condom?" I ask, wanting her to be comfortable.

"No, I'm on the pill." Fuck, I was hoping to get her pregnant, and have a little Nic or Nikita running around.

"Fuck her, baby boy. Make her come all over your fat cock. Then, when she does, come here, so I can get a taste."

Nic wastes no time positioning himself between her legs. Gripping his cock and lining the head up with her hole, he pushes slowly in. He's taking his time with her and it makes me hot.

As I watch him fuck her, I stroke my cock faster, knowing neither will last long. Nic from being deprived of coming and Carla, from what I can tell, it's probably been a while since she's been with someone.

Watching Nic thrusting in and out of her while he whispers words of affection makes me want to take him from behind, but I don't.

"Daddy, I'm going to come," Nic cries, asking for permission.

"Not before Carla. Sweetie, I want you to rub your clit as Nic fucks you."

"Yes, Daddy," she moans.

The sound of skin slapping skin sounds out throughout our room. The smell of sex fills the air and damn if it isn't my favorite scent.

They both cry out their release, and I increase my own strokes, following right after, ropes of cum shooting onto my hands and down my pants.

Nic stays sheathed inside Carla's pussy as they both ride out their high. Standing, I head to the bathroom, taking a washcloth from the rack and clean myself before stripping out of my clothes. Rinsing the rag, I head back to the bedroom, where Nic has just freed himself from Carla. I clean him up before turning to our girl.

"Nic, I know I told you I wanted to taste Carla on your cock, but I've changed my mind." Leaning down, I flatten my tongue and lick up the length of her folds, catching both of their cum as it escapes from her hole. Once I've got my fill, I take the rag and clean her.

"Time for bed," I order them. Helping Carla up, I pull back the comforter, before helping her into the bed. Nic kisses me deeply, then gets in beside her, with me taking the empty spot on the other side.

I fall into a blissful sleep. Life couldn't get any better.

CHAPTER SIXTEEN

NIC

Waking up with Carla between us this morning feels right. Like she was always supposed to be here, with us. Now we just need to convince her to make that permanent. I'm already planning how we can redecorate the spare room for her son, until we can build a bigger place, one for our family to grow old in.

Carla's snoring very faintly, but I'll never tell her that. She's rolled on her side toward me with her hair fanned out on the pillow and her mouth opened ever so slightly. I swear she looks like an angel.

Chad props himself up on his elbow, his fingertips sliding down the length of her torso, over her hips, and down her legs. Once he goes as far as his arms will allow, he traces them back upward. A motion that would be so relaxing if you were awake.

"She's perfect for us. You were right to love her for so long, Nic." His voice is barely a whisper, so he doesn't wake her.

"Are you sure you want to add her to what we have?"

"Without a doubt, Nic. I love you more than words can ever say. Even if she says no, I will die a happy man, having you. You're the first love of my life. One I will have until my dying breath and then for whatever comes after. Nic Santini, you are my everything. But Carla, she will be the missing piece that will make us a complete unit. We can both admit we have enough love in our hearts for her, her son, and the many children to come." He sits up, leans over her body, and crashes his lips on mine.

Her soft whimpers underneath us tell us she's awake and very much affected by us kissing. So I deepen it, capturing Chad's mouth forcefully, which is normally how he kisses me. He lifts his free hand, running his fingers through my hair, taking hold of my head. Holding me tightly, he pulls back from the kiss and begins nipping on my bottom lip, before biting down hard.

My cock twitches at the pain, and I want more. The taste of Carla last night was not enough to ease the need within me.

His hand remains, holding my head, but he leans down and takes Carla's mouth with his. Kissing her deeply while I watch. She rolls onto her back as she rubs her thighs together. I know she's feeling the same need as I am. Reaching out, I push the blanket down, exposing her pussy to me. I let my fingertips glide across her stomach and down, slipping between her folds, running tiny circles along her little nub.

She moans and fuck, my cock throbs.

Chad releases her mouth, staring intently at her, then at me.

"Carla, I want you to ride my face while Nic sucks my cock. Can you do that?"

"But I'll smother you. I wouldn't even know how to do it?" She panics a little, her eyes wide.

"Oh sweet girl, what better way to die than being smothered by your sweet little cunt as I drown in your juices? Now, I'm going to get on my back and I want you kneeling over my face. I'm starving," he tells her and damn if I don't agree. It would be the sweetest death ever, only comparable to choking on Chad's fat cock.

Chad does just as he says, and Carla looks over at me, almost hesitant, scared.

"It's okay, sweetheart. Let him taste how amazing that pussy of yours is. He only got a tease of it last night when he licked you. Not near enough, in my opinion."

"Y-y-you're okay with it?" It's then I realize what it is. She's worried I will think negatively of her.

"Of course. You're ours, if you'll have us. We want you one hundred percent."

It's all she needs to hear. She comes up on her knees, straddling Chad, and moves up so her sweet pussy is right over his face. She holds onto the headboard as she lowers down on him.

She lets out a long, drawn-out moan and I know he's going to town on her. "Rock on his face, sweetheart. Take what you want from him. He wants to give the world to you." Just like a pro, she grinds her hips against his face.

I take a moment to relish in the sight. The girl I've loved and wanted for years with the man that holds my heart. It's perfect. My eyes trail down his body, stopping on his rock hard shaft. Taking hold of it, I open my mouth wide, sliding down over his mushroom head, pausing only to relax my throat. He was blessed with both length and girth, making both me and Carla very lucky.

Chad bucks his hips up, pushing more of his shaft into my mouth. Reaching down, I take hold of my own dick, fisting it as I pump up and down in rhythm with my head bobbing.

My moans vibrate off of his cock as Carla cries out in pleasure. I can feel my balls tighten and tingling in the pit of my stomach and I know I'm close. I increase the speed of both my sucking and pumping, wanting so badly to taste Chad's sweet release.

I don't last much longer, as hot ropes of cum shoot from my cock, coating my hand and the sheets. My eyes look to the right as I hear Carla cry out in pleasure, gripping her legs tightly around Chad's head, I know she's found her release as well, and it's all Chad needs before I'm swallowing down all the warm, salty goodness he has to give me.

After the last drop, I clean him with my tongue before pulling off with an audible pop and licking my lips. Helping Carla off his face, we all collapse in the bed, worn out, and drift back off to sleep, held tightly in each other's arms.

Carla

My eyes blink open slowly, a bright light shining in through the partially opened curtains, right into my face. Looking to my left and right, I see both of the guys are still asleep, and slowly shimmy my way out of their hold so I don't wake them.

Once I'm out of the bed, I look back down at them, as they gravitate closer to each other, Nic rolling on his side, as Chad spoons him from behind. A smile covers my face as I bring my fingers to my lips. The touch of their soft lips, still tingling like an echo moving through a cave.

The need to pee wins out and I make my way to the bathroom. Once I'm done, I wash my hands and look at myself in the mirror, my hair a wild and crazy mess like I stuck my fingers in a light socket. I need a shower, a change of clothes and coffee. All in that order. Well, maybe the coffee first. Lifting my arms, I rake my fingers through my hair, trying to calm my angry waves into something just a little more manageable.

I see the guys' toothbrushes and toothpaste sitting on the bathroom counter. Picking up the paste, I put some on my finger and brush my teeth and tongue, ridding myself of my awful morning breath. Chad kissed me with my breath smelling like this. Yuck!

Stepping out of the bathroom, I look around the room, spotting my underwear and dress on the floor. I need to get dressed and go home. I've never done a walk of shame before, but it looks like I will be this morning.

I've dressed, and they haven't moved an inch. Picking up my purse and shoes, deciding I'll put them on in the hallway, I head for the door. This wasn't a mistake for me, but I don't want to face them when they wake up and realize they made one. The rejection would be too much. But at least I got one amazing memory to carry with me for a lifetime.

Taking hold of the door handle, I begin to turn it.

"Where do you think you're going, baby girl?" comes from behind me in a deep, gruff voice.

Turning to look, I see both Chad and Nic sitting up in bed, staring at me, both with confusion and maybe a little hurt on their faces.

"Home." One word, that's all I have.

"Why? Have you changed your mind?" Nic asks, his voice cracking as he speaks.

"No. God no. I just didn't want to be here in case you changed yours. The fear of rejection is just too much and I need to change clothes, anyway."

"Oh, Carla. Baby, you're not getting away from us that easy. Like we told you last night, you are ours. You're the missing puzzle piece in our life." Chad sits up in bed, reaching his hand out for me to join them.

"Really?" I let go of the door, taking slow steps toward them.

"Yes. Now, let us all get showered and dressed. We'll run by your house and you can get clothes for tonight and tomorrow, and then we will find some coffee and food." Chad's strong, commanding voice tells me, while Nic just nods in agreement.

"Okay."

CHAPTER SEVENTEEN

CARLA

I managed to convince Chad and Nic to stop and get food first, then drop me off at my apartment. Not only did I apparently need to pack an overnight bag, but I also missed Brandon and wanted to spend a little bit of time with him. The guys wanted to meet him, but I just wasn't ready for that. Not yet anyway.

Both guys got out of the SUV, placing a chaste kiss on my lips, letting me know they'd be back in about an hour and a half for me. I watch as they get back inside and drive away, then turn and head inside my building.

Trudging up the steps, I decide to go to my apartment first, then go see my little man.

What I wasn't expecting to see was Jack standing at my door.

"Well, if it isn't the slut. I was just about to leave, thinking you weren't here. This must be my lucky day." His sadistic voice sing-songs.

Steeling my nerves, I try to move past him to my door. The sooner I get inside, the better. Maybe not letting the guys come in was a mistake.

"I'm not a slut, Jack. What are you doing here, anyway?" I try to step around him, but he moves in front of me as we do a dance back and forth. Every time I move to get away, he steps in my path. "Get out of my way."

"Oh, I don't think I will. You think you're funny, slutting around with the two of them in front of me? Trying to make me jealous?" The way his words are almost slurred, you'd think he was still drinking.

"Jack, I think it's time you go. You lost all ability to control anything I do when you left me."

"Does he know?" he asks, letting out a maniacal laugh

"Does who know what?" Confused by what he's saying.

"Never mind. It'll all come out in the wash, and then I'm going to sit back and laugh. Tell your little fuck buddy if he touches me again, I'll bust his fucking teeth in. He won't look so good on the camera then." He reaches out, brushing his fingers along my face, and I flinch as memories come rushing forward.

Jack senses my moment of weakness, snatches a handful of my hair in his hands, and shoves me into my door. His hand comes up, cupping one of my breasts and squeezes hard. "Maybe if you play your cards right, I'll take this stretched out cunt of yours one last time. Remember what I said, Carla." He lets go of me, turning and walking away, disappearing down the stairwell as his laughter echoes out.

I fumble with my keys, finding the one for my door, and quickly unlock it and step inside. Slamming the door behind me, I turn the deadbolt, ensuring it's locked and I'm safe inside, before sliding down the door until my ass hits the floor. Then and only then, do I break down.

He's fucking crazy, and it's like in that moment I was teleported back to the past, where he controlled every aspect of my being. One where I lived in fear of whether I would live or die after one of his beatings.

I don't know how long I sit there, but I eventually pull myself up. He's gone. I'm safe, and I swore I would never let that asshole have power over me again. Sitting on the floor in a panic is doing just that, giving him power.

Making my way to my bedroom, I open my closet, reach up on the shelf, and pull out my small overnight bag. I rifle through my dresser, hopelessly looking for my nicest, sexiest lingerie and sadly come up short. Lingerie hasn't been a necessity and with no one to see it, there really wasn't a need for it. I finally decide on a pair that somewhat matches and is void of any holes, along with a nightgown and a pair of socks. Pulling out the next drawer, I get a pair of jeans and a shirt.

The only thing left I'll need is my dress for tonight. It's a black cocktail dress, nothing fancy, just semi-casual enough for the event. It's one of the few things I have left from when I was with Jack, so while his memory taints the dress, it's all I own. I fold it neatly and put it in the bag with a pair of heels. Last, I just need my deodorant, perfume and makeup and I think I'm done.

Once I'm packed, I double-check it for anything that may be missing before pulling out an extra pair of jeans and a shirt. Slowly pulling off my dress and underwear from last night, I toss them into the hamper and quickly redress in some clean clothes. Checking my phone, I see I still have about thirty minutes before they'll be back and I would much prefer to be waiting for them on the sidewalk.

Putting the strap of the overnight bag over my shoulder, I head for the front door, picking up my purse and keys from where I abandoned them on the floor. Coming up on my toes, I take a look out the peephole, not wanting to walk into another Jack ambush and head to Martha's apartment to see my baby. One night away and I already miss him.

Lifting my hand, I knock three times on her door. I can hear the sound of footsteps on the other side, getting louder with each one, and I know she's walking to the door.

It flies open and the smile on her face drops. "What the hell are you doing here?"

"I thought I'd stop in and see Bra..."

"Mommy," his little voice squeals as he comes charging at me, wrapping his arms around me. "What are you doing here? Me and Aunt Martha were getting ready to leave to go to the toy store."

"I just wanted to stop by and say good morning before I head out for my own adventures today," I tell him happily as Martha glares.

"Brandon, sweetheart. Why don't you go run and finish brushing your teeth and getting dressed while your Mommy and I talk over some coffee?"

"Yes, ma'am," he calls out happily as he runs off, disappearing into the bathroom.

"So. What happened? And I want all the details." She gives me a wink as we head to the kitchen.

"Okay, cliff notes version. I went to the reunion. Met up with Nic and Chad. We had some drinks. They told me they wanted to be with me, that I was the missing piece to their puzzle and wanted to spend the rest of their lives with me. We had sex, went to sleep, woke up, had more sex, and now they are on their way back here to pick me up to spend the night with them."

"Holy fucking hell. Praise Jesus, you got your cobwebs cleaned out. God knows you needed a good oil change on that vagina. So they want to whisk you away and spoil you. I hope like hell you jumped on board that train. They seem like they're good people."

Then I tell her the worst part. "Jack was there last night. And just now he was at my apartment."

"The fuck! Where's my damn gun? I swear I'm going to shoot his fucking dick off," she grits out angrily as she slams her hands on the table.

"Don't, he's gone. You know he's married. Well, at least he's wearing a wedding band, and she is very pregnant. Do you think he treats her like he did me?" I pick the cuticle on my nail, not even looking her in the face.

"I don't know, Carla. But you're better off. I'm glad you got away from him when you did. That boy in there saved your life, and he doesn't even know it."

"What do you think will happen if he ever finds out I lied? That Brandon is his child? Do you think he'll try to take him from me?" It's always been my biggest fear.

"You didn't put him on the birth certificate, so how will he ever know? Honestly, he hasn't caused a stink about it and it's been seven years. I think you'll be okay." She leans in, giving me a hug.

"Okay, I'm going to tell Brandon bye. The guys are picking me back up and will be downstairs any minute,"

I tell her, as I slowly stand, readjusting the strap of the bag on my shoulder.

"Are you hiding Brandon from them?" Martha stands as well and asks.

"No. They actually want to meet him. Can you believe they want to be his father? Both of them. They want me and my son. I just think it's too soon to spring them on Brandon. I need to be sure they mean what they say." I can already feel the tear starting to fall and quickly reach up and brush it away. Last thing I need is for my son to see me upset.

"I have a good feeling about the two of them." She reaches out, giving my arm a squeeze.

"Brandon," I call. "Come, give me a hug goodbye."

He rushes out of the bathroom and I drop down on one knee, taking him in my arms and hugging him tightly.

"Mom, I can't breathe," he croaks out.

"I'm sorry," I tell him, pulling away as I let him go, only to reach out and muss up his hair with my hand.

"Moommmm. Stop!" he cries out in laughter.

"Okay, have fun and be good. I'll see you tomorrow." I give him a kiss on the cheek before standing up.

"Bye, Martha."

"Bye, Hot Stuff," she croons, and I just shake my head at her as I head straight for the front door and out of the apartment.

Just as I step out of the apartment door, a very familiar SUV pulls up to the curb. Nic jumps out, running over to me and takes the bag from my shoulder.

"I missed you," he tells me.

Fuck, he is so sweet. Why did I not act on my feelings for him in school? Oh yeah, that's right. Jack.

CHAPTER EIGHTEEN

NIC

"I missed you too. It seems weird saying that." Her voice is soft as she glances at me.

Taking her bag, I open the back door to the SUV for her to slip inside. She's quiet and looks pale. Is she getting sick? Did something happen?

She sits silently the whole ride back to the manor. I sneak glances at her in the rearview mirror, and I catch Chad doing the same. Carla hasn't looked up once, just stares at her hands in her lap as she fiddles with the hem of her shirt.

Chad and I keep glancing at each other out of the corner of our eyes, each of us filled with concern. If I know my man like I think I do, once we're safely behind the doors of our room, she's gonna be spilling the beans.

"Do you want to pick up something for a late lunch or just order in?" Chad asks, breaking the silence.

"Food sounds good. Maybe some subs. That way, if we don't want to eat them right away, we don't have to worry about them being cold," I add, but Carla never says anything. She just continues to sit there quietly.

"Carla?" Chad asks, when she doesn't answer.

"I'm not hungry." Her voice is flat, void of all emotion.

"You have to eat, baby." Chad's voice is strong and commanding.

But she doesn't answer. Just sits there. Until finally she speaks.

"Fine. Subs are fine."

Yeah, there's something wrong. This isn't the same woman we dropped off at her apartment this morning. The woman in the back seat looks as if someone has ripped her to shreds. And I intend to make whoever took the shine that was on her face this morning pay.

We run through the drive-thru of the only sub shop in town and then head straight for the manor.

"Nic, Carla. I'm sorry to say, but this town sucks. There's nothing here. We barely found what we were looking for when we went shopping today. Unless there's somewhere else, the Eagle's Nest seemed to be the most exciting place in town. What did you guys do as kids?"

"Well, I can attest growing up here sucked. If you were popular, there was the soda shop, games on Friday nights, parties, and the movies. But if you were me, the kid everyone picked on, you stayed home. Sometimes me and Lorna would just go to the park and hang out there. We found an old abandoned tree house and fixed it up. So we each used it as a hideaway. Me from the assholes at school and her, although school was its own hell, her home was far worse," I tell him, and I can see the way he cuts his eyes at me about that.

He's always known why I hated this town, but not Lorna. She kept her secrets close to her; only Kylo and I know the hell she went through at home. If I could murder her family, I would. Hell, I've looked into hiring someone, she just doesn't know it. What's it called? Deniable plausibility? Maybe? Only thing I knew for sure, if she didn't know anything, she couldn't be held accountable.

"Carla, what did you do?" Chad once again tries to coax her into conversation.

"Umm. I was normally at the parties, games, you know, what the popular kids were doing." Her voice is unenthused as she speaks.

We finally pull in at the manor, and Chad parks right in front. Turning off the car, we all get out and I toss the strap of Carla's bag over my shoulder as I take her hand. Chad picks up the bag with the sandwiches in it and we all head inside, tossing Gladys a wave as we go. *Does that woman ever sleep? Or is she a vampire? I mean, I haven't seen her go out into the sunlight yet. So it's possible.*

Once we're inside the room, Chad's had enough. He puts the sandwiches on the table and glares at Carla. She hasn't even noticed. Her attention elsewhere.

"What happened?" I ask, trying to be a little more tactful than Chad.

"Nothing," she whispers.

It's a lie.

"Carla," I say again, adding some inflection to my words.

"Really nothing. I'm just tired," she says again.

Still a lie.

One I will not be letting her get away with.

"Carla, you and I both know that's not true. So I'm giving you a moment, then I expect the truth." Chad's forceful, dominant voice booms through the room.

She lets out a huge breath of air, then the tears start to flow. Running down her face uncontrollably.

"It was Jack."

"That douche from last night? What did he do? Where was he?" Questions fly from Chad's mouth.

"Chad, calm down," I tell him, noticing Carla is getting more upset by the minute.

"Tell me about you and Jack. I know there was some strain in school. He used to beat me up all the time for talking to you."

"He did?" Her face pops up, looking at me, her eyes wide with surprise.

"Yeah, all the time. What happened after graduation? Why are you still here? Weren't you planning to go to some college in North Carolina? What was it, ECU?"

"Yeah, I was hoping to go there, then apply for their Physical Therapy program. But Jack didn't want me to leave. He didn't get into any of the schools he applied to, so we went to the local community college."

"So you went to college, just not where you wanted. How did you, and please don't take this the wrong way, end up working at a diner?" Chad asks. But in actuality, we both want to know. She was so smart, she would've dominated being a therapist.

Doctor Carla Sanderson. It has a nice ring to it.

"He flunked out of school. Then he made me quit." She's sobbing now, each word labored.

"Carla." She lifts her head to look at me, tears rolling down her face. "I need you to answer my question truthfully. Did he hurt you?"

She looks deep into my eyes, pleading with me not to ask, but I hold fast with my gaze. I need to know.

Chad paces behind me the longer she goes without answering. Looking up at him, I see him rubbing his fisted hand in the palm of his other one. He's going to blow like Mount Vesuvius.

"Carla." Reaching out, I take her hands in mine as I lower down onto the floor, kneeling in front of her. I'm ready to be her support. Her rock.

She can't answer verbally, but she gives us a nod.

He's dead.

I'm going to kill the motherfucker.

A long, agonizing death.

"Why is he calling you a slut?" Chad asks this time.

"When I found out I was pregnant, I knew I couldn't stay in the relationship with him. He always accused me of cheating, but I never did. I couldn't. Even if I wanted to. Not when he always had eyes on me. I was a prisoner in our home."

"So, how did you leave?" I ask.

"I was a couple months along when he found out I was pregnant. When he accused me of the baby not being his, I went along with it. It was a blessing in disguise. A way out. He wanted to know who the father was, but I never told him. Before he left me, he beat me so badly I had to be taken to the hospital. I almost lost Brandon that night."

"HE'S FUCKING DEAD!" Chad booms out into the room.

"No, please. I can take it. He can call me anything he wants as long as he stays away from Brandon."

"What did he do today that upset you?" I already know I'm not going to like the answer.

"He was at my apartment, waiting for me. Jack accused me of being with you to make him jealous.

Like I'd want to do that. He said he was going to spill everything tonight. I'm not sure what he meant by that."

"Is that it?" I stroke her hand with the pad of my thumb.

"He told me to tell Chad that if he touched him again, he'd bust his teeth in." Chad bursts out laughing at that. Hell, so do I.

"Let the asshole try," he barks through the laughs.

But there's one more thing I need to ask. A piece of me already knows the answer. But I can't go another minute not knowing.

"Did he touch you?"

She nods her head and all hell breaks loose.

The crashing of a chair rings out through the room as Carla jumps in fear.

I pull her into me, whispering calming words to her as she shakes in my arms. Looking over my shoulder at Chad, I give him a glare.

"Get it together or leave until you do. You're upsetting her more."

Chad's eyes go wide. Realization hitting him at the scene he caused as he looks at the fragments of broken wood on the floor. A mental reminder not to go barefoot until we get this cleaned up and vacuumed.

Chad rushes over, dropping to the floor beside Carla. "I'm so sorry, baby girl. That fucker will never lay a hand on you again. Not while you have Nic and me in your life, and believe me, we aren't going anywhere. You're stuck with us."

We stay like that, a huddled pile, while Carla goes through all the emotions she's hiding inside. Only when she has calmed do we sit down to eat. She doesn't eat a lot, but enough to appease the daddy in Chad that she won't starve.

"Okay baby, both of you. Strip and in the bed. I want you both to take a nap while I go handle paying for the broken chair, and arranging to have a maid come up and take care of cleaning the room while we're out."

And just like the good boy and girl we are, we do just as he says.

CHAPTER NINTEEN

NIC

Chad's voice stirs me from my slumber.

"Fuck yeah. I love the idea. I've always wanted to own a sports team. I'll buy it under the name of my photography business and list Nic as a silent partner," I hear him say.

Cracking open my eyes, as the room comes into view, I see him sitting in the chair, feet propped up on the other one as he talks on his phone.

"I'll send all the information to my lawyer and sign the paperwork on Monday. Mums the word until you're ready to make it public. Just one thing; promise me I can be around when the shit goes down. I want to see their smug ass faces when you spring it on them." He's quiet for a moment and I know the other person must be speaking until he finally tells them goodbye.

"I know you're awake, Nic," he calls out, making sure to keep his voice low. Carla needs her rest.

Pulling myself from her arms, replacing my body with the pillow, I slowly get up, making sure to stay quiet and pull on boxers. Walking over to him, I sit down in his lap, wrapping my arms around his neck and kiss him.

"Who was on the phone and what are we buying?" Curiosity is getting the better of me.

"Just helping someone out and making us some money in the long run. I'll let your best friend explain that."

"Okay," I answer nonchalantly. There's not a thing I wouldn't do for Lorna. As far as friends, hell, people go, there's none better than her.

When I think of what she went through and the people who allowed it to happen, I get sick. I know there's no way in hell I could have survived it and come out sane. How she did, I'll never know. Those fuckers deserve every bit of revenge she throws at them, and I hope they burn in hell.

He places the palm of his hand on my thigh, rubbing gently up and down the length. "Are you ready for tonight?"

"No, but I'm gonna do it, anyway."

He skims the back of his fingers along my jaw, causing my body to shiver. Chad always has that effect on me.

"I love you." His words come out of nowhere, filling me with warmth.

"I love you, too. One of the best days of my life was meeting you in that library."

The rustling of sheets pulls our gaze over to the bed. Carla is waking, stretching her arms above her head as she lets out a long yawn.

"I haven't slept that good in so long." Her face is twinkling with joy. Carla hasn't smiled like that since before she got with that tool Jack, in high school.

"Good. It's getting late. Who's ready to shower? We have a night of dancing and reminiscing to get to," Chad says happily, placing his hand on my leg and rubbing, adding a squeeze at the end. "I have a surprise for the two of you once you're done."

The pleased smile on his face, and the way his eyes are lit up, make me both shiver with anticipation and maybe just a smidge of fear.

"Did one of you want to go first?" Carla asks, her voice soft and meek.

"Why don't the two of you take one together? Nic can help you wash your hair. While we were out, we stopped by the store and picked up some toiletries for you," Chad says as he helps me to stand.

"You didn't have to do that." She brings her hand to her heart, almost as if the small gesture of buying her some shampoo is the biggest thing someone has done for her lately.

"We know, but we wanted to. Spoiling you and your son will be the highlight of our day," I tell her.

"And I may have purchased a few more items for you." Chad's grin is mischievous now and even I'm wondering what he picked out when he disappeared for twenty minutes.

"I don't know what to say." The sobs threatening to come out muffle her words.

"Thank you. That's it. Now Nic, why don't you take Carla to the bathroom and the two of you get showered?" He gives me a swat on the ass that has me jumping both in surprise and from the sting.

Walking over to Carla, I take her hand in mine and help her out of bed, leading her to the shower. The only thing I wished at this moment was that I had a view of her ass like Chad did.

Thankfully, the best part about the reunion was it was in the ballroom of the manor we were staying in. When we're ready to leave, we simply walk back to our room. No need to wait for a ride to come pick us up.

Both Carla and I gasped when we saw Chad's surprise and our asses are now proudly dawning a jeweled butt plug. He no doubt wants us ready for whatever tonight may hold. He not only had that but a vibrating cock ring for me and Carla's panties now hold a small vibrator inside them, hitting right on that delicious clit of hers. Both devices are controlled by him.

Tonight is going to be fun.

A knock at the door pulls our attention and I head over to open it.

Standing on the other side are Lorna and Kylo. She is decked out in a dress even more seductive than last night. There are two men that are going to have raging boners all night.

Fuck that, all of them will. Hell, let's face it, the women will be creaming their panties as well.

"Damn, don't we clean up well, Nicky? Carla, you look beautiful." She steps inside the room, Kylo close behind her as she walks over and hugs her.

She's right, Carla looks simply gorgeous. She's wearing a wine red dress with a silver band along the bodice. It's sleeveless on one side, with long flowing panels of varying lengths that are higher in the front than the back.

While she was sleeping, Chad got her shoe size and had the dress shop deliver a pair of black sling back shoes along with the dress. How Chad got the right size for the dress, I'll never know. It must be a secret talent of his.

She's a goddess. One I hope spends the rest of her life with Chad and me.

"Are we ready to head downstairs and knock these assholes down a peg or two? I only want to be there as long as I need to," Lorna exclaims.

"Are you revealing yourself tonight?" I ask her, curious.

"Who knows? I'm going to let the chips fall where they do tonight. But I really hope your little investment goes off as planned, so I can hit them in the gut with it."

"We will know Monday." Chad winks at her. "I'll be sure either Nic or I call you as soon as we sign the papers."

She does a little shimmy dance and all of us burst out into laughter.

Kylo pulls her back into his body, flush against his front. Leaning into her, he whispers something in her ear. Whatever it is, it has her squirming underneath him at the same time a vibration hits me. It's so intense, my cock stirs.

My groan pulls everyone's attention, while Chad just has a devious look on his face.

"Man, I should have thought about that for you, Lo." Kylo's grizzly voice echoes through the room.

"Umm, that would be fun," her seductive voice rings back.

"Yeah, my babies have little surprises coming to them all night. If they don't come, they'll be rewarded later," Chad announces as my gaze trails over to Carla, who has a very red face.

"I'm sorry, sweetie. We're just very open about sex. I guess it's an aftereffect of the lifestyle we live." My heart breaks thinking we've embarrassed her in some way. Sometimes we forget others are not as open as we are sexually.

"I-i-i-it's okay," she stutters. "It'll just take some getting used to."

Getting used to; that's what she said.

Fuck yes!

It means she plans on being around us. She's giving serious thought to us as a throuple.

"Well, I guess we should get downstairs," Chad announces as Kylo takes Lorna's hand and leads her out of our room. Carla follows closely behind, but I stop Chad, needing a moment just to speak with him privately.

"Go easy on her tonight. She's not used to this." My eyes and words pleading with him to understand.

"I know, baby boy. Trust me. She just needs a little encouragement. A little exposure. I'll go easy on her." His tongue glides over his bottom lip. "But you, I won't." He gives me a kiss, then places his hand on my lower back, leading me out into the hallway where the others are waiting for us.

We head to the end of the hallway and push the button for the elevator. It doesn't take long before the doors slide open and we step on. There's a couple already on it, and they both look familiar.

I steal a glance over my shoulder until it finally clicks. Leslie and Trent. Looks like they did end up getting married. I always knew they'd make it and find their way back together. Good for them. They seem happy. I give her a small smile when she catches me looking, and she returns it.

Just a smile, nothing more. We don't need to speak. Even in school, we barely did. Only when we needed to. She was one of the nice ones, though, so I have no ill will toward her.

The ride to the floor that the ballroom is on passes by in silence. Guess all of us have our own feelings about this reunion. Carla takes my hand, squeezing it. I know she's anxious about running into Jack again tonight.

Chad told me about what he did to him at the bar while we were out shopping today and my only regret was not being there to kick him in his fucking face. I pity his wife and the child she is carrying. Her best bet would be to run from him and create a new life, just like Carla.

The elevator comes to a stop, and a few moments pass before the door slides open and we step off.

"Okay, Buffaloes. Are we ready to blow this motherfucker up?!" Lorna booms excitedly as we head to the ballroom.

Stepping inside, we halt for a moment, looking around, and I can already feel everyone's eyes on us. Somewhat different from how they looked at us while we were students. At least for me, it feels that way. I know they're all trying to figure out what I do? It's been a secret I think I've kept pretty well, that is, unless you've watched some of the movies I made. Which I'm sure there's a few in here who have.

Looking around, it's much like last night. The cliques from high school still banded together. There are tables set up around the room and tables laden with food with covered dishes and burners underneath them. There's a large screen in the front of the ballroom that has a projection program playing on it.

Who Are They Now? pops on the screen as it starts flipping through pictures of our graduating class from then and now, along with who they are.

Can't wait to see what mine says.

CHAPTER TWENTY

NIC

I see Olivia across the room and my face lights up.

"I'm going to say hello to Olivia real quick, since I didn't see her last night," I tell them.

"Okay, me and Kylo are going to steal your girl for a minute and grab some drinks. Meet us at the table?" Lorna tells me more than asks, as she takes Carla's hand into hers.

My heart swells with how Lorna has attached to Carla. Taking her under her wing, being a friend to her.

Leaning down, both Chad and I give her a kiss. "We'll be right over there." I tell her, pointing in the direction Olivia is standing.

"Okay," she mumbles softly, scanning the room, and I know she's looking for him. I don't want to leave her alone too long, so I need to make this quick.

The only thing keeping my anxiety at bay by being away from her is the fact that Lorna and Kylo would kill for her, knowing how we feel about her. She is one of us now.

Taking Chad's hand in mine, we head across the room to her. Her eyes meet ours, a huge smile on her face as I wrap her in my arms.

"Holy shit, I don't believe it. I knew you said you were coming, but I figured you'd back out," Olivia says with a laugh.

"You know Lorna threatened my life if I didn't come," I joke with her.

"I bet she did. So, I couldn't help but notice who came in with the two of you," she says slyly, her eyebrow rising.

"Yep. We're working on us," I say proudly.

It's at that moment Rhett decides to step up to us. I give him a death glare, much like the rest of the people around me.

He banters back and forth with Olivia, and even though she's trying to show an outward hatred for him, I sense more.

Chad finally breaks the silence and introduces himself. When Olivia and Rhett fall back into conversation, we take that as our opportunity to excuse ourselves.

The others have found a table, and we make our way over to them. I already see Lorna staring down two of our old teachers, and I see revenge in her eyes.

As soon as we get to the table, the two of them split up. Kylo heads in the direction of Rowan and Abel and Lorna walks toward our old instructors. This should be fun.

But I don't get to witness any of it. Suddenly a vibration hits me and I have to grip onto the table as I clench my jaw, riding out the euphoria. Catching a glimpse across the table, I see Carla in much the same predicament. She has such a glow and I love it.

Chad releases her from her vibration quicker than he does me, evident by the change in her body posture. I'm used to this type of foreplay while she isn't. But I can't wait for the day she craves it, just like me.

Her face is flushed, and she looks gorgeous. She looks around quickly, and I know exactly what she's doing, checking to see if anyone noticed. They didn't. If she had started to moan out loudly or wasn't able to stop her orgasm and scream, Chad would've stopped. He'd cover it up, so no one noticed, so she wouldn't be embarrassed.

As the time ticks by, many have come up to me to say hello and ask how I've been. Posers. The whole fucking lot, especially when none of them would talk to me in school. It doesn't escape my notice that no one talks to Carla. It's like she's not even here. A mere ghost.

I won't fucking stand for it. Looking at Chad, I see the anger flaring up in him much the same way about what's happening.

Finally, I've had enough.

Another old classmate, one who stood by and watched me be tormented and bullied all through school, steps up to the table with a fake smile on his face. Trying to schmooze and see what he can find out about the illustrious Dominic Santini.

"Hey, bud, so good to see you. How have you been?" he asks jovially as he reaches out and slaps me on my back. Chad tenses beside me at the movement, but I reach over, placing my hand on his knee, calming him.

"I've been great. I'm sorry, but I just don't seem to remember you," I say with a sanguine voice, pretending to be nice. Yeah, I know who the cocksucker is.

Jensen Michaels.

A follower of every asshole in this school, riding on their coattails to popularity. And on my list of the fuckers at this school I can't stand.

"This is my husband, Chad." Then I gesture toward Carla. "You remember Carla, don't you?"

I don't miss the look of disgust he gives her. Nor do I miss the way his eyes linger on her, staring at her chest. Mine and Chad's chest. She's ours.

"Yeah, I remember her. Honestly, I can't believe you're sitting with her after what she did to Jack." The hate in his voice is evident, even though he doesn't know the truth. Typical boys' club mentality.

"Excuse the fuck out of me. What *she* did to Jack? So we take what our buddies say and treat it like it's gold. When in reality he's scum. That's okay. Take your ass and move along. The only reason you came over here was to see if you could get answers to fill in the blanks about me," I bite out angrily, ready to punch this fucker in the face.

He steps back, not expecting the weak boy from high school to have grown a backbone. Yeah, that's right asshole, I did. I could beat your ass from one side of this room to the other and not break a sweat.

"Look, I just thought you didn't know about how she cheated on him and got pregnant with someone else's kid. Was going to save you, but forget it now, man." He throws up his hands in an 'I give up fashion' and walks away, headed straight for Jack and his pregnant wife. The aforementioned glaring daggers at us.

My eyes quickly shift to Carla, who's shaking. "Hey, baby, it'll be okay. I don't believe a word the fucker says," I tell her, trying to console her as I reach out across the table, taking her hand in mine. She's so shaken up, it's ice cold.

"Hey, pretty girl. You got us, so don't listen to these tools. We know who you are and we want you," Chad reinforces to her.

She just nods her head, fighting hard to hold back tears.

The night passes and we've had some food. The number of people coming by to stop and talk started to dwindle, especially when Lorna and Kylo returned to the table. Lorna excuses herself to the bathroom and Kylo goes to get another drink. With them leaving, I get up and move to Lorna's vacated seat beside Carla and claim it for my own.

It's not long after I see Kylo cornered in a heated debate with Abel and Rowan, and Lorna walking up behind them, anger and smug satisfaction written all over her face. At this moment, I wish I was a fly on the wall because I know it's finally going down. I'd heard the rumors about what Jack told them about her. Hell, our school was nothing but gossiping bitches, and that hasn't changed in ten years.

It's not long before she's leaving in laughter, dragging Kylo behind her as she tosses me a wave, putting her hand to her ear, letting me know she'll call me. Chad and I burst out laughing, while Carla looks between us, confused as to what just went down. She'll know soon enough; we'll share with her later.

Rowen screams, "Fuck you, Santini!" after he slams his drink down, mumbling something to Abel as he storms from the room.

I can't help it. Normally I would blow it off, but the devil sitting on my shoulder is whispering in my ear, telling me to let him have it.

"You certainly got fucked. You took what peace she should've had from her. You deserve everything you have coming," I yell back to him, loud enough for him and anyone near us to hear over the music as I wrap my arm around Carla.

"What just happened?" she leans in, whispering in my ear. Her warm breath hitting me and sending a beeline straight to my cock, as it jerks to attention in my pants.

"We'll tell you later," I whisper back.

I want to turn and look at her, but my eyes catch on the bastard across the way, totally ignoring his very tired, pregnant wife as he locks his gaze with mine. It's going down tonight, one way or another.

"I'm going to the bathroom, then I'll be right back." Carla goes to stand, but I take her by the hand, stopping her. Pulling her to me, I crush my lips onto hers, kissing her so deeply and passionately I can feel my toes curl like they write in romance novels, except I'm the guy.

When I release her, Chad does the same, and I know all eyes are on us. Good, it's not like it bothers me. But these assholes need to know if they disrespect our woman again, all hell will break loose.

"Hurry back," Chad tells her, giving her ass a swat when she turns to leave. She looks back, laughing, before heading on her way.

Chad waits until she's out of earshot before speaking. "Now that Lorna's gone, I'd say you fulfilled your obligation. Do you want to bust this popsicle stand and head back to the room?"

"I thought you'd never ask. You know just how to woo me, baby, by getting me out of this circus show." The laugh that rips from me is contagious, and Chad joins in with me.

We both pick up our glasses and drink. It's only when our glass is empty, it dawns on us how long Carla's been gone.

Something doesn't feel right. I get an icky tingling sensation in the pit of my stomach that runs all the way up my spine. Looking around the room quickly, I don't see her anywhere. But I also don't see him.

"Jack's missing and Carla isn't back. Let's go find her. I have a bad feeling." Chad quickly stands with me and we head straight toward the bathroom.

When we turn the corner, I see them both.

Jack has Carla pinned against the wall as he berates her and she's cowering underneath him. I can see the parts of her visible body shaking in fear.

This asshole is going to die.

CHAPTER TWENTY ONE

CARLA

I never in a million years thought ten years later I would be here in this town for a high school reunion again with Dominic Santini on my arm. Not only him, but Chad as well. Fuck, I don't even know his last name. Maybe that does make me a whore.

Stepping out of the bathroom, I run into a brick wall. One that causes me to stumble back into the bathroom door that's shut behind me. My head hits it hard as pain radiates down my spine.

"I'm sorry," I mumble out.

"Yeah, I know you are, slut," a familiar voice growls out, laced with pure hatred.

"Jack? Why are you doing this? We're not together anymore. It looks to me like you've moved on and from the ring on your finger and the very pregnant woman you're with, your life is great. Why continue to treat me this way?" My voice trembles as I speak.

"Because I can, you fucking whore. You were mine, and you dared to cheat on me? Now you're here with those two bastards. They're together, you know, or is your pussy so greedy one dick isn't enough?"

My jaw drops in shock. I knew he was like this, but the years apart must have dulled me some to the crass words he can spew. The venom that courses through his blood, waiting for the perfect moment to spill and poison someone else.

"Why are you like this?" I sound like a broken record and I know it, but it's all I can think.

"Because of you, cunt." His brazen words spew out of his mouth, his spit hitting me in the face, making me want to cringe.

"I never did anything but love you, Jack, and it was never enough. Nothing I did was ever right. You weren't happy with me, so why do you care that I had a child with another man? Especially since you always said you never wanted children. Why can't you let me go, or do you just love abusing women that much?" Tears are streaming from my face now. Terror wracking my bones at what's going to happen, and I feel like I'm right back in that spot I was in over seven years ago. The same broken girl he so easily manipulated as a teenager and into adulthood.

"Do you think I care about my fat ass wife? She did the same as you, got pregnant when she knew I didn't want a fucking kid. But I gotta make my parents happy. The bitch went and told them before me, or else she'd have had an abortion by now. She was just a filler, someone to take your place. A cheap replica," he spits out. It's only then a soft voice speaks up.

"That's what you think of me?" she asks, her eyes red from crying as she cradles her stomach.

"Get off your high horse, bitch. You knew how I felt. It's no fucking secret," he screams at her.

She breaks down, turning and racing down the hallway away from us. My heart breaks for her. Maybe she didn't know the demon who lived inside of him.

"Now, back to you. What do you think Santini and that man hanging all over him are going to think of you when they find out about your bastard?"

"He already knows I have a son. He and Chad both. So, go ahead and tell him if that's going to make you feel better." I reign in my emotions, not wanting him to see the effect he still has on me. I need to be strong.

"Does he now?" An evil grin escapes his mouth.

"Yes, he does, they both do. What's the big deal, Jack?" I practically scream at him, as I place my hands on his chest and try to push him away from me, with no success.

Tomorrow I'm starting a workout program. No longer will I be weak. Workout and self-defense are on my to-do list.

"You know what? You and them are a perfect match. While you give your body away for free, they sell theirs. Fucking anything with two legs and letting people watch. Imagine what kind of diseases they have. Fucking porn stars, that's what your loose ass pussy wants?"

"I'd suggest you step away from our girl right fucking now, Jack!" Nic's strong voice echoes down the hallway.

Peeking around Jack's body, I see Nic and Chad charging toward us, and I'm filled with both relief and dread. Can they take Jack if it were to come down to a fight?

"Oh, if it isn't the pansy-ass porn stars." Jack steps away from me as he swipes his thumb across his lip, laughing.

"Yeah, we make pornos. Are you a fan? Do you want an autograph?" Chad's words come out very flippant and nonchalant, but his eyes are laser focused on Jack, waiting for him to make a move.

"Carla, baby, come over here to me," Nic tells me, but fear still has me tethered to my spot. "Carla. Come on, it's okay. This jerk isn't going to do anything."

Then and only then do I move. Slowly creeping along the wall, moving away from Jack and closer to Nic, until I'm far enough out of Jack's reach that I practically leap into Nic's arms.

"She's really got the two of you pussy whipped. I know for a fact it isn't that great, but I'm going to do you a solid and tell you just how much of a bitch Carla is. Her kid, she tried to play it off as mine, but I know who the father is. And surprise, surprise, it's you, Dominic." He gloats as my heart plummets into my stomach.

How did he know I put Dominic's name on the birth certificate?

I take a deep breath, preparing myself for what's to come. Nic knows he isn't the father. There's no way he could be. Before this weekend, we had never had sex. Now Jack's going to know he's the biological father. Is he going to try to take him from me? It's something he would do. Fight me for custody just to be spiteful and make my life miserable, not because he actually wants to be in his son's life.

"I know. Why do you think I came back?" She came to me as soon as she found out. I was an idiot back then. Being a father wasn't something I was prepared for and instead of taking money from me, from us, she did everything on her own. We were the assholes in this, not her. So, if you think we're abandoning her because of that, you are sadly mistaken." Nic's powerful voice is loud and clear as he cradles me to his chest, the vibrations calming me.

"Nic, this scum isn't worth our time. Let's go," Chad says as he comes up beside us and guides us back down the hallway.

Scared is not a strong enough word to describe how I feel. Did Nic just say all that to save me some embarrassment? Time will tell. But my heart and mind are at war with what's going to happen once we can all talk freely.

We step back into the ballroom when Jack's words bellow out behind us.

"Sluts and whores, that's what the three of you are. Most successful, my ass. There isn't any way you're making money. There isn't anyone who wants to see two men having sex!"

"That's fucking it," Nic says through gritted teeth as he turns to face Jack. "Okay, asshole, you want it to all go down? Want everyone to know the truth? Well, let's get it all out there."

He hands me off to Chad, who wraps me up in his arms, acting as my protector. We're still on the outskirts of the room, but there's enough people standing around that whatever is about to happen will spread through the school like wildfire.

"Everyone! Listen up! I'm only saying this once because you don't even deserve that. This man standing here is my husband. We've been together for eight years and I love him more than anything. And for those wondering, I'm bisexual, so this woman, whom you all know, is our girlfriend, and if we have anything to do with it, she'll be our wife. Now, as far as the cheating goes, that is just inaccurate. Because she has been bullied, abused, and every other horrible thing you can think of by this prick since she started dating him in high school. He manipulated and controlled her and I regret every day that I didn't speak up sooner and save her from it. She didn't cheat, they had nothing, and I'm the father of her son. And damn proud of it."

He pauses, looking around, making sure those around us are paying rapt attention.

"This prick of a man spread lies and every one of you believed just because the almighty Jack Hendricks said it. Even stood by this whole weekend as he treated her like shit. Now me, yeah, I make porn with my husband as well as others. It paid my way through college and made me a fucking millionaire who owns his own business, clubs, and some new investments." I can hear the gasps echo out.

"Yeah, you heard right. I'm a fucking millionaire. So, Brighton High School, you wanted to know who we are now. Well, that's it; Dominic Santini is a husband, boyfriend, father, porn star, CEO of his own businesses and a fucking multi-millionaire. I'd dare say the most successful person out of our graduating class. A class that deserves no more of my time or attention." With that, he turns, kisses Chad and then me before taking us by the hands, leading us from the ballroom out into the hallway.

All I can see are the dropped jaws of everyone around us and as I look up at the screen of our graduating class, I see the sweet graduation picture of Nic looking back at me. No other picture or information about him is listed, but by the end of the night, everyone will know exactly who he is now.

"Nic, I can explain," I tell him, tears streaming down my face.

He stops at the elevator, pushing the button. Neither he nor Chad say anything.

It's over. I know it. He doesn't need to say anything. I'll get my things and call Chip to come and pick me up.

The elevator door slides open and Nic stands inside, bringing me with him as Chad steps in behind us.

Still nothing.

It's so silent, you could hear a pin drop.

My anxiety and fear only rise when the elevator door slides shut and he pushes the number for our floor. He squeezes my hand, sending me mixed emotions. Is he comforting me? Why did I let Martha talk me into coming to this thing? Giving me their number? I should have just thrown it away and continued on with life as it was; Nic, a glorious memory from my past.

The elevator comes to a halt, bouncing a little when it stops, causing me to lose my balance momentarily and fall into Chad. His arms reach out, catching me and steadying me. Looking up at him, I see him staring intently at me. But his eyes don't hold anger, they hold love.

Once again, we step off the elevator and head to our room. It's only when the door is opened and we step inside that Nic pulls me into his arms and kisses me so passionately I can't even process what's happening. Chad steps up behind me, his lips peppering kisses along my neck, until he reaches my ear, trailing his tongue along my ear lobe as heat pools in my center.

Is this just one last time before they cut me loose? I don't think I can do it. To have them once more, to only say goodbye. I need to get myself under control and not let my hormones rule me. We need to talk about what happened. Nic needs to know why Jack thinks he's the father. I'll assure him I will remove his name from the birth certificate. It won't be much; a simple paternity test will prove he's not the father. Just something else for all the assholes in this town to look down on me about.

CHAPTER TWENTY TWO

NIC

Carla pulls away from us, breaking the moment. "Please, just let me explain," she whispers.

It hits me–she must think we're mad. But that's not the case at all. I don't even need to converse with Chad; I know he feels the same way as me.

"Carla, sweetheart. Why would we be mad?" I ask, wanting to give her a chance to answer. I step toward her, but she takes a step backward and I halt in my spot. She's skittish right now, and I need to be patient.

"Because I lied and Jack told you."

"Can I ask a question?" Chad asks, and she nods her head.

"Why does Jack think Nic is the father?"

"I don't know how he found out. When I found out I was pregnant, it was during the time you were here for your father's funeral. I kept it a secret and when I couldn't hide it any longer, I told him I cheated. When Brandon was born, I put your name on the birth certificate," she explains, and it clicks then.

"Oh, sweetheart, that's how he found out. Birth certificates are public record. Anyone can get that information." Her shoulders slump at my words as her legs give out and she starts to fall. Chad is closer to her and catches her before she hits the floor, and helps to carry her over to the chair.

"I'm so sorry I lied. That you told a lie to protect me. I'll make sure everyone knows the truth." She can barely get the words out.

"But they do know the truth," Chad tells her, causing her to whip her head up in confusion.

"No, they don't. I mean, I didn't cheat on Jack. That was a lie, but Brandon is his. I just couldn't let him be born into that world. To be raised by that monster."

We both move over to her, kneeling down in front of her. Each of us places a hand on one of her knees.

"Baby. You never lied. Everything I said was the truth. When Brandon was born, I wasn't ready to be a father. But now I am. Both Chad and I are, and as far as Brandon, well, all he ever needs to know is I'm his father. When he gets older and asks, I'll tell him the same thing we told every asshole in the room who was in earshot of our conversation. He's our son. And when I said I hoped you would one day be our wife, I meant that too." She stares at me with wide, red-rimmed eyes.

"Nic's right. You legally having your son as Nic's is a sign. We're destined to be together and we'll take all the time you need, but know that we want you and Brandon with us."

"You do?" She blows out a breath of air.

"We do," I reemphasize to her.

"Now, I need the two of you undressed and standing in front of me." Chad stands from the floor, removing his jacket and laying it over the back of the empty chair. Angling it towards the bed, sits down in it.

Standing, I can't erase the smile from my face. I've got my man, my woman, and a son. This reunion has turned out to be amazing and I'm going to have to suck it up and thank Lorna for making me come. She's never gonna let me live it down, either.

Carla still looks a little shell-shocked, her eyes wide, and a look of disbelief on her face, but she does exactly as Chad says. Tonight we bask in each other; tomorrow we plan for our future. I know in my heart, without a shadow of a doubt, that Chad has the same plan in mind.

Once we're naked, Chad gives us an approving look as we stand before him, eyes down, hands clasped behind our backs. He rests his right elbow on the chair as he takes his hand and strokes along the goatee of his chin, exposing his Adam's apple to us as his lips part slightly.

"Sit on the edge of the bed. I want to look at both of you while you pleasure yourself," his suave voice commands us, and we eagerly obey.

"Nic, be patient for a moment. Carla, take your fingers and put them in your mouth, suck on them, then run them through your folds before stopping on your clit, stroking your fingers back and forth across it. Don't be quiet. I want to hear you pleasure yourself, how good you can make yourself feel."

She lifts the dainty fingers of her right hand to her mouth and when she sucks on them, all I see is her lips wrapped around my cock. If I wasn't hard before, I definitely would be now.

She lowers them, letting them slide through her folds, her breathy moans filling the room, as the tips of her fingers glide along her clit in circular motions. Her legs fall open, exposing even more of her glistening pink pussy to us.

"Baby boy, I want you to take two of your fingers and thrust them in and out of her hole, coating them with her juices, before spreading them along the shaft of your cock. Then fist it and show me how you like to give yourself pleasure."

I'd rather have my face buried between her legs, but it's not what he wants. Doing exactly as he says, I begin to finger fuck her, making sure to curve the tips of my fingers as I pull out and stroke them across her G-spot, bringing her closer to her climax.

"No, Nic, she doesn't get to come yet. Now spread her sweet juices all over your cock and let me watch you play." He lets out a small guttural moan at the end as he undoes his pants. Pulling out his dick and gripping it with his hand, he does nothing more, just holds it as he watches us.

Sliding my hands along the length of my cock, I spread her juices, and when pre-cum begins to leak from my slit, I run my thumb over it, mixing it with her essence. I don't know how much longer I'm going to be able to last with Carla beside me, making all those intoxicating sounds and Chad in front of me, gazing at us with such intensity. If he said come, I would.

"Good. You're both divine. Now lie back. Time to take out those plugs. Yours was just to start prepping you, Carla, because soon that ass will be ours and one of us will be taking you in each hole at the same time. Stuffing you full of our thick cocks."

He stands slowly, slipping out of his shoes as he slides his pants down his legs, until they pool at his feet and he steps out of them. Stepping closer, he begins to unbutton his shirt, then slowly pulls out his arms, one at a time, dropping it to the floor. Standing before us, my mouth begins to salivate at the sight. His chiseled abs, those muscular thighs, and can we talk about those pecs? He's the perfect mix of muscle and softness and thank gods this man is mine. I'd kill a bitch to have him. Thankfully, I don't have to.

He squats down on the floor between Carla's leg, running his nose up her slit as he inhales deeply. "One of my favorite smells," he growls, before running his tongue between her slick folds. His hand literally tip toes up the length of my thigh before he places it over mine. Grasping my cock, he strokes it in sync with eating our woman out.

The smell of sweat and sex fill the room, and no one has even been fucked yet. Chad looks up from between her legs, his face covered in her juices. He comes up on his knees, moving closer to me. Taking his hand off my dick, he moves it to the back of my head and pulls me to him, cutting the distance between us. Only when I'm within a hair's distance of his face does he crash his lips on mine, forcing his tongue inside my mouth.

"She tastes delicious, doesn't she?" he asks me once he releases me, the corner of his lip quirking up into a grin.

I almost nod, but catch myself. "Yes, she does."

"I'm going to fuck her now. I'm going to fill this tight little hole of hers with my fat cock, and make her come all over it," he tells me as he taps her thighs lightly. "Move up the bed, sweet pea."

She brings her legs up on the bed, digging her heels in as she pushes her way further up. "On your knees, Carla. Nic, I want you in front of her. She's going to suck your cock like no one but me has before."

Carla quickly turns, getting into position as I move in front of her, my back against the headboard. All she needs to do is open her mouth and take me in. Chad moves in behind her and I peek over her shoulder. He gently massages her ass and lower back before taking hold of his dick, lining the head of it up with her hole and thrusting inside of her.

She lets out a guttural moan. The familiar sound of when he enters and your hole has to stretch to accommodate his size. I would know it anywhere.

"Fuck, baby, you're gripping me like a vice. Now take Nic into your mouth and make him feel good."

She opens her mouth, sliding down on my cock and begins to bob her head up and down. My hand instinctively reaches out, slipping my fingers through her hair. Gripping it tightly, I begin thrusting up into her mouth at the same time Chad thrusts in and out of her.

I can feel her moans and gasps vibrating straight through my cock. She is sucking it so good; I know it's only a matter of time before I'm filling her sexy little mouth with my release. The sound of skin slapping and her slurping fill the room.

"Chad, I can't hold it anymore. I'm going to come," I cry out, desperately needing my release after all the teasing I've endured tonight.

"Then come, baby," he tells me as I catch a glimpse of his hand moving to Carla's ass, rubbing a finger around her butt plug before pulling it out. She gasps and moans at the same time, kicking me right over the edge, and ropes of hot cum shoot down her throat.

Her body begins to quiver as her breaths turn ragged around my cock. Chad continues to pump in and out of her until he thrust one final time, grabbing hold of her hips and squeezing tightly.

We stay like that for a few minutes, connected in such an intimate way. Chad pulls out of her slowly, then guides her down to the bed, before bringing his gaze back to me, his cock already hard again.

"Now it's your turn, baby," he growls.

Reaching for my legs, he takes hold of them and pulls me closer to him until my crotch meets his. He lifts my legs up, pushing them toward my head. "Hold on to them," he orders with such authority, my hands whip up to take hold of them.

His hand snakes between Carla's legs, catching the mixture of both their releases and scoops it up. With his other hand, he reaches down, grasps my butt plug, and pulls it out before rubbing the mixture around my rim. His finger slowly slides in, one, then two, before he scissors them back and forth, stretching my hole even more.

His eyes are full of lust as they shift back and forth between me and Carla. In one swift motion, he pushes his cock in, filling me completely. There's no slowness to it. No, it's fast and forceful, exactly how I like it. Chad speeds up, brutally fucking me like a man possessed; his rough thrusts relentless, and the pounding doesn't stop until he's shooting his hot cum inside of my tight ass. Fuck, I'm going to feel that tomorrow and I will love every minute of it.

"I love the two of you. I'll be right back, so I can clean you up, and then we'll sleep. Tomorrow we'll talk about us and where we're going. Because make no mistake, Carla, you are ours." He stands slowly and heads to the bathroom, his bare ass flexing with each step.

I reach my hand out, taking Carla's in mine, as sleep takes over. Not even able to stay awake to see the glorious view when Chad returns.

CHAPTER TWENTY THREE

NIC

"So, how are we going to handle this?" I ask as we all sit around the table at the diner Carla works at, having breakfast. She needs to head home tonight to be with Brandon, so she can take him to school tomorrow. It's his last day, and he's having an awards assembly. Chad and I had hoped to convince her to leave, but we had to get an earlier flight in the morning after we got a call from the attorney about the new investment Chad and I have.

"I don't know," she pauses, looking between us. "Brighton has been Brandon's whole life. Everything he knows is here. I can't just uproot him without knowing what we are. If we're going to last." Her voice is soft, her eyes down.

"Okay, we take it slow. Time for you to get to know us. And so we can get to know our son. Because make no mistake he is. That birth certificate will never be changed. Chad and I can fly back and forth, then when you're ready, we can fly both of you out to see us, so we can look for a house. One large enough for the four of us and all the other kids we're going to have." She listens to every word I say.

She doesn't speak, just clears her throat before picking up her glass of water and taking a sip.

"We're also going to be adding you to our accounts. Use them to get anything you and Brandon need. Once you're living with us, I want you to think about college. I want you to go back and get that degree you want," Chad adds, as the color drains from her face.

"No, I can't let you do that. I don't want you for your money." Her voice rises as she speaks.

"We know. That's one thing we love about you. But you're with us now and you will never struggle nor want for anything," Chad reaffirms.

"And if you don't, well, we'll just get it for you," I add.

She looks back and forth between the two of us. I can see the wheels turning in her head as she thinks about everything we've said.

"Okay," finally slips from her full pink lips.

I want to jump for joy, scream to the heavens, but I keep my composure.

"But isn't that a lot of traveling for the two of you?" she asks, a slight tremble in her voice.

"I'd travel the world to be with you, Carla Sanderson." And I mean every word.

We spend the rest of breakfast planning each visit. In two weeks, we will be back in Brighton to meet Brandon for the first time. Then in a month they're coming out to spend a week with us. Little does she know we'll be taking that time to look at new homes. It's also when we plan to take her to one of our clubs.

With all the video calls and traveling, we're going to be some tired people. But it will all be worth it.

Before we know it, Carla is hugging us, and it's taking everything in me to keep it a respectable goodbye. But because of where we are, I keep it PG, much to my disappointment.

The ride back to the manor is quiet. Neither of us speaks, already feeling her absence.

Chad's rough hand comes down on my leg. "It won't be long. This is short-term. They'll be with us soon. We just need to be patient."

"I know, it's just hard. After all this time, to finally have her, only to leave her behind. It feels wrong." I lean my head against the car window, watching as the town passes by.

The flight home was long, and we finally made it, but instead of heading home, we went straight to the attorney's office. Pulling up to his office, we quickly head inside.

"Chad, Nic. Good to see you. I know you've just flown back in, but you said this sale was a priority," the attorney says as he reaches out, shaking each of our hands.

"No problem, Sam. Our friend will be happy to hear the sale is complete once we leave here. It is stated in the paperwork that SanMat LLC is the owner. You have me listed as the CEO and Nic as my silent partner?" Chad asks as we step inside his office and take a seat in front of his desk.

"All your specifications were handled to the T. All you need to do is sign here and here on the contract and then we can authorize the payment transfer. Then you are the proud new owners of a hockey team."

Twenty minutes later, we're headed out of the office and I send a text. Just two words.

Me: It's done.

A string of smiling faces and knife emojis, among other things, follow, sending both Chad and me into hysterics.

"Well, guess we have another trip to add to our travel plans." Chad winks and I shake my head at him, smiling.

"I can't believe it. The reunion I dreaded going to has made us complete and richer." Disbelief still consumes me. I have to pinch myself to know it's real and that I'm not going to wake up to find it was just a dream.

"It's only up from here, baby. Just a few months and they'll be here. With us. And we're never letting them go. I have to make a confession, though. I called the diner while you were in the restroom at the airport and Martha answered. She's on our side and will be letting us know what Carla needs, even when she doesn't. First thing on the list is a car. Apparently, according to Martha, Carla's car is held together with duct tape and a wish. How do you feel about doing some car shopping online once we get home?"

"I love it. You know, I really liked the SUV we rented for the reunion. It's spacious and safe."

"Plenty of room for more kids. I'm not lying when I say I've been praying she ends up pregnant." He laughs.

EPILOUGE

NIC

Six Months Later

Today's the day. Not only did Carla and Brandon move here, but our new club is finally opening. We ended up firing the architect and starting over fresh and it was the best decision we ever made. It took longer in the end to get it built, but it was well worth it. Our new architect not only saw our vision but turns out was also part of our lifestyle. A win for us, in my opinion.

We're headed to the ribbon cutting tonight and Chad's cousin is coming in to watch Brandon while we celebrate the grand opening. I tried to convince Carla we could hire a nanny, but she didn't want to leave him with someone new after they just arrived today. It was an act of congress just to get her to agree to Sandy doing it. Carla only caved and agreed because it was Chad's cousin.

"Okay, I think I'm finally ready!" she calls loudly from the bathroom.

"Then come out and show us." Chad and I decided to wear the suits we wore to the reunion, kind of in honor of our six-month anniversary.

When she steps out, our jaws drop and we both begin to drool over the woman before us. She's wearing a wine red dress, form fitting, with a slit up the side, so if she moves in just the right way, her beautiful pink pussy will be on display for everyone. The front drops into a deep V down to her belly button, putting her beautiful breasts on display.

I'm fucking hard.

Looking to the left, I see Chad is as well.

"Okay, we need to get this done and get back home. I want nothing more than to unwrap this beautiful package you dressed up in." I stride across the room, cutting the distance between us and wrap her up in my arms as I take the kiss I've been dying for.

"As much as I want to throw you on the bed and fuck your brains out, the car is downstairs. We just need to cut the ribbon, then we can leave," Chad tells us, causing us both to pout.

"None of that. Downstairs now!" He steps out the door and heads down the stairs.

Carla and I follow after him, finding him in the kitchen with Sandy and Brandon. The latter two are busy making ice cream sundaes for their movie night.

"Alright, little man, we will be back later, but you should be fast asleep." I step up to him and give him a kiss on his forehead before tousling his hair.

"Okay, Daddy," his chipper voice rings back.

When they came to visit, he had a lot of questions and we took the time to answer them all, sticking to the story we told at the reunion. We came to a decision that one day, when he's older, we'll tell him the truth if he asks, while hoping he doesn't. As far as he's concerned, we're both his dad, but I'm his biological father.

We all say our goodbyes and hurry outside, climbing inside the limo that's taking us to the club. Lorna and Kylo are meeting us there, along with some surprise guests.

The ride is filled with nerves. Tonight we have a major announcement and a huge question to ask. And what better place than our new club?

Arriving at Carla's Desire, the driver pulls up out front where a crowd has already formed, all eager to see the inside. The three of us head straight for the front door, which is roped off with a huge green ribbon.

"I need to tell you something," Carla whispers loud enough for us to hear.

"Can it wait?" I whisper back, as the attorney steps forward to hand Chad a microphone and a pair of the biggest scissors I've ever seen.

"No, I've kept it a secret for two months now, and well, I can't hold it in any longer." She looks between the two of us, both of us furrowing our eyebrows in confusion.

"I'm pregnant," she pauses as what she says sinks in, "with twins."

Chad swoops her up in his arms, swinging her around before quickly setting her back down, taking the microphone and big ass scissors from our attorney. "Oh my god, I'm sorry! Are you okay, baby girl?"

"I'm fine," she answers through laughter.

"Twins, really?" I ask.

She just nods her head as the biggest smile crosses her face.

"It's time to start," Sam tells us and we step in front of the crowd.

I take the microphone from Chad and look back over to Carla before I speak.

"Good evening, everyone. As many of you know, but for those who don't, I'm Nic Santini and this delicious man to my side is Chad Matthews, my husband. We had a chance encounter back in college, where he led me to awakening the sexuality I kept buried away from the public. It wasn't because I was embarrassed, I just came from a town where it wasn't spoken of. Together we thrived in the adult film industry, then formed our own production company."

A round of applause comes from the crowd.

"From there, we opened a string of BDSM clubs, which is why we are all here today. Our newest one is named after our newest partner. This beautiful woman in the red dress was one of my friends from high school and it took until our ten-year reunion for us to finally get the nerve to act on our feelings, thanks to my husband, a meddling best friend, and a co-worker of hers. Please step up, Carla."

Her eyes go wide, not expecting to be put into the limelight.

"She gave us some pretty amazing news tonight that will spoil ours. Seems she is making us fathers again, to twins this time."

The crowd begins to holler congratulations as she steps up. Both Chad and I go down on one knee, as I hold out a box in front of us. She covers her mouth, knowing what's in the box and what we're about to do.

"Carla, I have loved you since the first day I saw you. Never once did I stop thinking of you," I start, then Chad picks up.

"Nic always told me stories of you, and I knew you were special. It wasn't until I met you that I realized you were the missing piece to complete our puzzle."

We turn and look at each other before saying in unison.

"Will you marry us?"

She breaks down in tears and nods her head as she rushes out, "Yes."

I slide the ring on her finger and stand, hugging her tightly, followed by Chad, before he takes the microphone from me.

"Not to waste your time any longer, and seeing how Nic and I want to celebrate with our new fiance, we wanted to share our news with you all first, before the press release goes out. You may have noticed over the last few months, the only movies that Nic or I have starred in have only been with each other. That would be because of the beautiful lady who just said yes to us. But as of today, we will no longer be starring in any movies. We've decided that part of our lives has come to an end. Now I am happy to bring you Carla's Desire, our largest club to date, with over twenty private scene rooms, areas for scenes to be viewed publicly, a private area for our littles, and basically anything under the sun you could think of." Chad steps up the ribbon and cuts it, handing the scissors and microphone to Sam.

"Okay, ladies and gentlemen, you heard it here. It's a sad day for the world of adult films, but a day to celebrate the engagement and future birth that is to come. So please proceed and check out Carla's Desire," Sam announces as he holds the door open and the crowd enters.

"I'm ready to go celebrate. Let's go to the nearest hotel," Chad whispers, taking our hands as he heads to the car that brought us here.

Ten years after graduating from Brighton High School, I never thought I would be where I am today, this happy, and with two people who impacted my life in such different ways.

THE END

WHO ARE THEY NOW?
A BRIGHTON HIGH SCHOOL REUNION

BRE ROSE

Up Next in the Brighton HS Reunion Series...

Up In Smoke by Cassie Lein

Ten years ago the assholes at my school voted me the 'class clown'.

My outfits and behavior didn't fit the status quo of our upscale town.

They demanded to be in the spotlight while I enjoyed melting into the darkness.

I wrapped myself in things they deemed sinful, turning it into a mask to hide the

secret of my home life from others.

Escaping the hell I called home, I was able to make a name for myself.

Even if that name also keeps me hidden behind a mask.

Although, it's much different than the one from my childhood.

I may not have the career, family, or life that my peers 'grew' up to have, but I'm happy with what I've made of myself.

Even if it's not as fancy or glamorous as this town demands.

With my BFF at my side, I show up at my high school reunion with new secrets to hide. This time they involve the duo who made my life a living hell for four years.

I have one goal; ripping off the mask and striding into the limelight, revealing all the secrets.

I can't wait to see their faces when their idealistic life goes up in smoke.

Welcome to Brighton's High School Reunion, where revenge is on the menu tonight, and I'm one hungry bitch.

Check the Content Warnings/ Tropes

Sex Toys

Cam Girl

Past Child Abuse

Past Child SA (off Page)

Dubcon

Hidden Identity

Domestic Violence

Revenge

Hockey

Suicide

Blackmail

Acknowledgements

As always I want to thank my amazing family, both blood and not. My three boys, my besties and the amazing book community that surrounds me.

I want to send out a special thank you to all the authors who were part of the Brighton HS Reunion. I've enjoyed all our talks in the chats and sharing our amazing stories with each other, finding ways to make them interconnect.

To my Alpha and Beta team, thank you for all your help in making this story so amazing. I loved every bit of feedback that you gave me.

To Cassie, thank you for being my friend and for allowing our characters to be the best friends I know we are. Ones that never ask questions and are always there to support each other, even when we want to go on a killing spree (just in books, not real life - just making it clear) lol.

To my ARC teams, both for my solo work and for the Brighton series. You rock.

Shayna, my PA. What would I ever do without you? You know how much I love you, even when I know I drive you crazy. I know I can be a needy bitch.

Lastly, to the readers. Without you, I would be nothing. Thanks for taking a chance on my crazy ass and reading what pops out of my head.

To all the high school reunions to come!!!!!

About Bre Rose

Bre Rose writes under a pen name in both the contemporary and paranormal why choose genre primarily, but does have works that are MF. Bre is a native of North Carolina and mother to three amazing sons and two feline fur babies more affectionately known as her hellhounds.

She's always been an avid reader then progressed to becoming an ARC, BETA and ALPHA reader for some of her favorite authors. After some encouragement she decided to tackle writing the stories in her head and is loving every single minute of it. When she isn't reading or writing she enjoys traveling the world and still has some places to mark off her bucket list. She also enjoys spending time with her family and advocating for the differently abled population.

To keep up to date with all upcoming releases and all things Bre then simply join her facebook reader group Bre Rose Petal Readers.

Also By Bre Rose

Memphis Duet
Finding Memphis (Book 1)
Saving Memphis (Book 2)
Memphis Duet Omnibus

Memphis Spinoffs
Unbreakable
Memphis Beginnings:Novella

Prophecy Series
Shay's Awakening (Book 1)
Shay's Acceptance (Book 2)
Shay's Ascension (Book 3)

Beyond the Pack Series w/ Cassie Lein
Rise of the Alpha
Destroying the Alpha
Claiming My Alpha
(Coming June 2023)

Brighton High School Reunion Shared World
Reuniting With Desire
(coming July 2023)

Fairytales with a Twist Shared World
Charleston Curse

Merciless Few MC Shared World
Kentucky Chapter
Sinner Choice
(Coming August 2023)

Printed in Great Britain
by Amazon

30633242R00175